"Who are you?" Vict͏ raspy voice.

"My name is Aaron Shetler. You are on my property," he stressed, but she made no move to lower the weapon. "Can you put the gun down, please? My son is here."

Her gaze sped past him to where Caleb stood stock-still and scared to death.

Tension filled the space between them. She pulled in a breath. Let it out. Then lowered the weapon but didn't take her hand off it.

"What's your name?" He kept a careful eye on the weapon clutched in her hand. "Who shot you?"

Suspicion flared again in her eyes. "Why do you want to know?" That she didn't trust him was easy to see, though being shot would no doubt make one untrusting.

"I'm only trying to help." For the longest time he wondered if she would answer.

"Victoria. Victoria Kauffman." He scarcely caught the name. Her voice was but a whisper. She tried to sit up but couldn't. Falling back against the floor, she dragged in several breaths. "Some bad men are trying to kill me."

Mary Alford was inspired to become a writer after reading romantic suspense greats Victoria Holt and Phyllis A. Whitney. Soon, creating characters and throwing them into dangerous situations that tested their faith came naturally for Mary. In 2012 Mary entered the speed-dating contest hosted by Love Inspired Suspense and later received "the call." Writing for Love Inspired Suspense has been a dream come true for Mary.

Books by Mary Alford

Love Inspired Suspense

Forgotten Past
Rocky Mountain Pursuit
Deadly Memories
Framed for Murder
Standoff at Midnight Mountain
Grave Peril
Amish Country Kidnapping
Amish Country Murder
Covert Amish Christmas

Visit the Author Profile page at Harlequin.com.

COVERT AMISH CHRISTMAS

MARY ALFORD

LOVE INSPIRED SUSPENSE
INSPIRATIONAL ROMANCE

LOVE INSPIRED® SUSPENSE
INSPIRATIONAL ROMANCE

ISBN-13: 978-1-335-72204-1

Recycling programs for this product may not exist in your area.

Covert Amish Christmas

For questions and comments about the quality of this book, please contact us at CustomerService@Harlequin.com.

Love Inspired
22 Adelaide St. West, 40th Floor
Toronto, Ontario M5H 4E3, Canada
www.Harlequin.com

Printed in U.S.A.

There is no fear in love; but perfect love casteth out fear: because fear hath torment. He that feareth is not made perfect in love.
—1 John 4:18

For my editor, Dina Davis. Thank you for all that you do.

ONE

She never could sleep. No more than a few hours, anyway. Not since the attack.

Too many uninvited guests roamed around in her head, reminding her of the bad things she'd done in the name of justice…and the distance she'd traveled from her innocent upbringing because of them.

On the kitchen counter, a battery-powered radio played Christmas music. Victoria Kauffman stared out the window at the predawn darkness surrounding her rented cabin. Even though she couldn't see it now, the snow-covered landscape beyond the black brought back childhood memories of Christmases past. Good memories. Simple ones.

At one time, she'd lived an almost idyllic childhood among the St. Ignatius Amish… until that fateful year soon after her fifth birthday, when she'd lost the woman who meant the whole world to Victoria. Her mother.

One sweet memory in particular snaked out past the garbage in her head. All she could think about was that final Christmas before her mother's passing. Lately, she found herself longing for that simple way of life more and more. Back before she became a stone-cold killer.

Outside, the darkness moved. In an instant, her deadly past had her firmly in its clutches. She ducked low, her heart peppering out a frantic rhythm. There was no doubt in her mind. The men she'd been hiding from were out there.

A heavy object slammed against the front door, forcing Victoria into action. She grabbed her cell phone and tucked the Glock that once belonged to her partner, David, behind her back. The weapon had been her constant companion this past year. Partly because it reminded her of him, but mostly because it was one of the most accurate weapons she'd ever shot and practically indestructible.

There would be no time to retrieve the metal box containing the precious little evidence she'd hidden underneath the floorboards in the living room.

Someone rattled the back doorknob close to where she stood. Victoria ducked low and skirted past the door. They were moving in for the kill. Her survival was now measured in minutes. If she didn't come up with a way out that didn't involve the two main exits, she'd be trapped inside the tiny cabin. She wouldn't get out alive.

The window in her bedroom offered her only chance. If she could make it out without being caught, the wilderness surrounding the cabin went on for miles. She had the advantage. She knew the woods like the back of her hand.

So far, the door was holding under the weight being thrown at it. That wouldn't last.

Victoria carefully eased the bedroom door closed and slid the lock in place. It would provide little resistance for someone determined, but it might buy her some extra time.

She stepped up on the bed. A nerve-wracking squeak froze her in place. She listened carefully. They were still trying to break through the doors.

Nothing but darkness appeared through the parted curtains. Her sigh of relief was short-lived. If these men were CIA, like she believed, it was possible they'd anticipate her next move and be waiting. She certainly would if it had been her mission.

Too many cold Montana winters had glued the window shut. Victoria shoved as hard as she could. It groaned open an inch or two. The sound grated along her spent nerves. She braced and pushed it up the rest of the way.

Getting through the opening wasn't easy, but she swung her legs over the windowsill. Darkness stretched out below. Though the ground sloped, the drop should be manageable.

The front door gave way, followed a second later by the back. No more time. She jumped and hit the ground hard. Her legs buckled beneath her. She steadied herself with her hands, but the landing hadn't been a quiet one.

Hurry! She had to hurry. It wouldn't take them long to realize she'd gone out the window. Victoria jumped to her feet and ran toward the silhouetted trees.

"She was just here," an angry male voice barked. "Find her. She can't be far."

Victoria stumbled over the snowy ground. Her cover was blown. She'd done everything possible to keep her identity secret, and yet they'd found her again.

How? Her thoughts tumbled over themselves. She'd rented the cabin using her former last name. No one at the CIA knew about her Amish past. The real-estate broker who'd drawn up the paperwork cautioned Victoria the place had no electricity or running water. It was isolated by the mountains on one side and the West Kootenai Amish community on the other. She'd rented in the dead of winter, where freezing temperatures could be lethal, because the massive amounts of snowfall would alert her to anyone snooping around. She hadn't seen a single person since she'd moved in. Until now.

Her ragged breath fogged the air in front of her. Snow filtered through the trees above, covering her clothes. Prickly pine branches slapped her arms and face while the darkness surrounding her felt almost physical. The cold penetrated through her flannel shirt that was no match for the biting December freeze.

"Over there! I see her," a voice behind her yelled.

Falling back on her training, Victoria zigzagged through the trees as a hail of gunfire kicked up the snowy ground near her feet and snapped off branches.

This was life or death now. Outnumbered by far too many, it would be all over if they caught her.

An uneasy silence settled around the woods. Goose bumps sped up Victoria's arms. Before she had time to catch her breath, World War III exploded around her. This time, one of the shots hit its mark. The bullet seared through the flesh in her leg, and she bit back a scream as hot lead burrowed in deep. The momentum of the shot thrust her forward, and she came close to losing her footing, but somehow kept her legs beneath her.

Not like this. She couldn't die without knowing the reason for the attack that claimed so many lives, including David's. He was the love of her life, and she'd promised to find the truth no matter the cost—even if it meant her own life.

Blood soaked her jeans within a matter of seconds. Burning pain poured down her leg with each step. She could feel her body slowing down.

Flashlight beams danced all around, narrowly missing her. She ducked behind a tree. Waited. After a handful of tense seconds, she inched away from the tree enough to see that her pursuers were moving in a different direction. Though she'd lost them for now, as soon as they picked up her blood trail and footprints in the snow, they'd come after her full force. She had to keep moving.

A light appeared through the clearing in the trees up ahead. A house. Her relief was short-lived. This was Amish country. The house would no doubt belong to an Amish family. She couldn't bring her troubles to them.

The blood loss was taking a toll. If she didn't stop the bleeding soon, she could lose consciousness.

Victoria ripped off the bottom of her shirt

and secured a strip of cloth like a tourniquet above the wound.

Some distance from the house lights, a massive structure loomed through the snowy predawn morning. A barn? Maybe a workshop of some type?

Her weary body craved rest, but that wasn't possible. She'd stay long enough to secure the wound as best as she could and warm up. Then she'd keep moving.

She reached the building and squinted through the falling snow. So far, the men hadn't picked up her trail. Desperation sank in. For half a second, she debated reaching out to her former CIA commander, Robert Jamison. If she pulled Robert into her trouble, would they come after him?

In the past year she'd moved half a dozen times. Through each change, she'd been careful not to divulge her location and Robert never asked. If her association brought harm to the man who had been a father figure throughout her career with the CIA, she couldn't bear it. Unless there was no other choice left, she wouldn't contact Robert.

Next to the entrance of the building a sign read Shetler Family Furniture Makers. The place belonged to an Amish family.

Finding the door unlocked wasn't a surprise.

Most Amish were trusting and didn't lock their doors. Victoria twisted the doorknob and stumbled across the threshold into what appeared to be a single cavernous room. The scent of cut wood mixed with lemon oil permeated the space. A lantern hung near the entrance, matches beside it.

She struck one and touched the tip against the wick. Soon the lantern's warm glow scattered the immediate darkness around her. A smaller room was off to the right. Probably an office. The space she was in now had no windows, but several roll-up doors.

She held the lantern high. A long wooden worktable covered most of one wall. There were several power tools there. A diesel compressor nearby would power the tools since most of the Amish did not believe in modern conveniences like electricity.

Wood shavings blanketed parts of the floor near a dresser and bed. Victoria cleared off a space on the floor to set the lantern. She dropped down beside it and sucked in several breaths. She was running on fumes for energy. It took all her strength to rip the jeans away from the gunshot wound.

Her vision blurred. She tried to stay focused long enough to clean the wound and wrap it properly, but the loss of blood—and the time on the run—was too much for her weary body. She lay back against the shavings. The past year since David's death had taken a toll, but if she was being honest, the life she'd lived—the things she'd been forced to do in the name of justice—had chipped away at her soul little by little well before that.

A tear slipped free. David. He was always close in her thoughts. He'd fought so hard to make sure only she found the evidence. Somewhere among those photos was the key to bringing down people responsible for so much carnage. If only she understood what he'd been trying to tell her.

Aaron Shetler gripped the edge of the table. Quiet had returned to the countryside once more. A short time earlier multiple gunshots had interrupted the family's silent prayer.

"It's probably Samuel chasing off that rogue bear again," Aaron assured his *mamm* and his thirteen-year-old *sohn*. "I'll check around outside once the meal is finished. No reason to worry." Yet Caleb continued to watch the window in the living room as if expecting someone to appear there at any moment. He hadn't touched his plate.

"Finish your breakfast, *sohn*. We have much work to do today."

The boy's attention snapped to his father. With a tiny nod, he picked up his fork and dug into the breakfast casserole.

The only noise at the table was the silverware clinking, yet Aaron's troubled thoughts were screaming out a warning. It was far too late in the year for hunters, and it sounded as if there were more than one shooter. He didn't believe this was connected to his neighbor, Samuel Wyse, or the bear that had killed one of Samuel's cows last week. This was something else entirely. Something bad.

He swallowed the last bite of his food and scraped back his chair.

Caleb jumped at the sound. "Where are you going?" His frantic gaze sought out his father's for reassurance.

"To take a look around outside." Caleb rose as well, but Aaron stopped him. "Stay here with your *grossmammi*. I will be back soon." The boy's disappointment was clear, but Aaron wasn't about to put his *sohn* at risk until he knew what he'd be facing out there.

He carried his plate to the sink, washed it and placed it on the dish rack to dry. Crossing the room, Aaron grabbed his jacket from the peg by the front door and shoved his arms inside. He snatched the lantern and clamped his hat down low on his head.

A blustery wind swirled snow all around. Christmas was but a few days away and winter had the countryside firmly in its frigid clutches.

Aaron surveyed the silty predawn darkness. Nothing but wilderness stretched out beyond his fields. Lights in the distance confirmed several people were moving through the woods. An uneasy feeling settled into the pit of his stomach. Whoever these people were, they were looking for something. Or someone.

He stepped from the porch and searched around the house. Finding nothing out of place, he went back inside, where *Mamm* and Caleb waited. Both anxious.

"Is everything *oke, sohn*?" The lines engraved on his mother's forehead ran much deeper than this moment. She'd suffered much loss in her life.

"*Jah*, it is fine." He patted her arm. Though his doubts wouldn't allow him to believe it for himself, he couldn't pile the additional burden onto her.

"Caleb, help your *grossmammi* clear the table. I'll bring the wagon around so we can get an early start." The dresser and bed set, made from the best lodgepole pine milled by his brothers, was almost finished. He'd spent weeks painstakingly creating each piece. All that was left was the stain and it would make a fine addition to young Turner Zook's home when he married his bride come next November.

As he stepped outside again, he did his best to push aside his mounting concerns. Something troubling was going on near the woods. Perhaps once the work was finished, he'd stop by Samuel's place to see if his neighbor knew anything.

In the barn beside his house, Aaron led the mare to the work wagon and quickly harnessed the animal. The simple tasks were what he found the most comforting these days, a constant he counted on to never change.

With the task finished, Aaron led the horse into the cold morning. He hopped up to the bench seat and shook the reins. The mare's breath steamed the air as she clomped through the snowy yard to the house.

Caleb must have been watching through the window because as Aaron neared, his sweet boy stepped out onto the porch. The light from the lantern in Caleb's hand highlighted how much he resembled his *mamm*. Irene's hair was that same rich brown color.

Of all the tragedies his family had suffered, losing his precious wife was the hardest to accept. It had devastated him.

All your fault... His conscience was always there to taunt him with the truth.

Caleb climbed up next to him and noticed the

lights. "Look, *Daed*. Do you think those people were shooting at the bear?"

Aaron buried his guilt down deep and focused on his *sohn*. "Perhaps." Yet he didn't believe it. There were far too many of them.

The drive to the workshop was filled with Caleb's enthusiastic chatter. Like Aaron, the boy loved his life here in the Amish community of West Kootenai, Montana. Though the work of a furniture maker could be hard and long at times, Caleb never complained. One day, Aaron looked forward to his *sohn* carrying on the family tradition alongside him and Fletcher, much like he and his brothers had.

"*Daed*, can we see if we can find the bear ourselves?"

Aaron kept his attention on the path ahead. "Perhaps. If we get the work done early." Going into the woods would allow him to look around. Maybe he could figure out what the men were really searching for.

As they neared the shop, Aaron reined the mare to a halt. He jumped down and reached for the lantern. Before Caleb had a chance to follow, Aaron spotted something that had him whirling back to his *sohn*.

"Stay where you are." His voice was filled with apprehension with *gut* reason. The workshop door stood ajar. Aaron stared at it for a full second while a chill chased between his shoulder blades. Something more than Turner Zook's furniture waited for him inside.

As he headed toward the open door, he spotted something alarming in the snow—blood drops leading straight into the building.

Aaron dashed to the wagon and grabbed the shotgun he kept for chasing off aggressive animals.

"*Daed*, what's wrong?" The fear on his *sohn's* face made Aaron question the wisdom of staying. Was he putting his child's life in danger?

"Nothing… I'm not sure. Stay here."

Aaron covered the stretch of ground to the door while all sorts of possibilities chased through his head. None welcome.

The lantern kept near the door was missing. Aaron stepped inside, his eyes darting around the workroom. The lit lantern was in the middle of the room. He started toward it and realized someone was lying on the floor near the light. A woman. She wasn't moving.

Her braided, pale blond hair was flung across one shoulder. She wore jeans and a torn flannel shirt. No jacket, despite the freezing December morning.

His uneasiness only increased when he noticed what appeared to be a gunshot wound on her leg. Blood seeped from the fresh injury. The shots he'd heard earlier flew through his head. Had the people he'd seen combing the woods shot this woman? Why?

From the amount of blood on her jeans, it was clear she'd lost a lot already. Scraps of material matching her shirt were tied haphazardly above the entry point. She'd tried to stop the blood flow but hadn't been successful.

His hands shook as he dropped to his knees and felt for a pulse at the base of her neck. Weak but there. Nothing in his life had prepared him for dealing with someone who had been deliberately shot.

"Is she dead?" Aaron whipped toward the sound of his *sohn's* voice. He should have known Caleb's curiosity would get the better of him. He'd warned the boy on many occasions about the pitfalls of being too curious.

"I don't know." Aaron turned back to the unconscious woman. "Hold the light for me, *sohn*." He handed the lantern to Caleb, removed his jacket and pulled out his pocketknife. Aaron cut away a strip of lining.

The woman's jeans were torn above the knee, where the bullet had ripped through the material. He removed the pieces of her shirt that acted as a tourniquet and fastened fresh strips of lining to cover the wound itself, before loosely securing them. When he finished, he slipped his jacket back on.

"Let's get her to the wagon. She needs a doctor right away." While Aaron tried to work out the best way to move the injured woman, a whisper of sound had him turning toward her.

Aaron stared down the barrel of a gun. The sight of it had him sitting back on his heels. All he could think about was Caleb's safety. Her hand didn't seem at all steady. One false move and he'd be dead. His shotgun was out of reach. If she intended to use the weapon, he'd never reach it in time.

"I mean you no harm." He sought to assure her while keeping his hands where she could see them.

She didn't blink. Didn't lower the weapon. He thought about the lights he'd seen earlier. What had she done to make these men come after her?

"Who are you?" she asked in a raspy voice.

"My name is Aaron Shetler. This is my family's building. You are on my property," he stressed, but she still made no move to lower the weapon. "Can you put the gun down, please? My *sohn* is here."

Her gaze sped past him to where Caleb stood stock-still and scared to death.

Tension filled the space between them. She

pulled in a breath. Let it out. Then lowered the weapon but didn't take her hand off it.

"What's your name?" He kept a careful eye on the weapon clutched in her hand. "Who shot you?"

Suspicion flared again in her eyes. "Why do you want to know?" That she didn't trust him was easy to see, though being shot would no doubt make one untrusting.

"I'm only trying to help." For the longest time he wondered if she would answer.

"Victoria. Victoria Kauffman." He scarcely caught the name. Her voice was but a whisper. She tried to sit up but couldn't. Falling back against the floor, she dragged in several breaths. "Some bad men are trying to kill me because of something I may have witnessed. Or know." She shook her head as if trying to work out the truth for herself.

Aaron's eyes widened. "Something you witnessed. Where? How?" He couldn't imagine such a scenario.

"While on a mission."

A mission. Who was this woman?

"Look, I know how strange this sounds, but it's true." She paused long enough to cast a look his way. "I once worked for the CIA, that's the Central Intelligence Agency. It's a government agency that gathers intelligence around the world for security purposes. I was on a mission in the country of Afghanistan with my partner and several other CIA agents when we were bombed. Everyone on my team died except for me." She stopped. Her face revealed the pain was still fresh.

Aaron struggled to grasp what she'd told him. This woman was some type of spy. He'd heard stories of such people but couldn't understand the world in which they operated. Terror threats. Wars. None of that was part of his existence.

"These men who shot you, they were the same ones who attacked your people?"

She confirmed with a nod. "I'm certain of it."

His attention dropped to the bullet wound. One thing became clear—whatever this woman was running from, she'd brought her troubles to his door. He wasn't sure what to do about that. "They are the ones in the woods," he said to himself.

Before she could respond, a disturbance outside pulled away his attention. Voices. More than one.

Victoria struggled into a crouching position. "If they find me, they'll kill me. Who knows what they'll do to you. I shouldn't have stopped here."

No matter what, Aaron couldn't let her leave on her own. After losing so much blood, she wouldn't stand a chance against the amount of manpower he'd seen in the woods.

The voices grew closer. Right outside the door now.

"You are in no condition to go anywhere," Aaron said in a low voice. "Let me see if I can get rid of them, then I will take you someplace safe." He rose. "Stay with her, Caleb."

With his *sohn's* confirmation, Aaron headed for the door. Before he opened it, he glanced back. His *sohn* had moved closer to Victoria, in a protective way that warmed his heart, despite his worry for the boy. Though still young, Caleb was becoming an honorable person. Irene would be proud. He certainly was.

Aaron slipped through the opening and closed the door behind him. Before he had the chance to move, four armed men drew their weapons on him.

"That's far enough," a man said in a sharp voice.

Aaron started to raise his hands and realized they were covered in her blood. Instead, he tucked them inside his jacket and waited for his heart to slow to normal. Being on the business end of a gun twice in a matter of minutes was unsettling.

The man who'd spoken looked him up and down, then visibly relaxed. "Put your weapons away. He's Amish." Like the rest of his team, the *Englischer* was dressed in dark clothing, and had a knit cap pulled down low on his head. He appeared to be in his forties and was clearly the leader of the group because the rest of the men obeyed and holstered their guns.

"I apologize for startling you. My name is Mike Logan. My men and I are federal agents. We're searching for a fugitive." He took out his phone and brought something up on it. "Have you seen this woman?" Logan held the phone so Aaron could see. The woman in the photo was the same one who waited inside with his *sohn*. Had he left Caleb with a wanted fugitive?

"What did this woman do?" Aaron asked instead of answering properly. Something about Logan's behavior put him on alert. He didn't believe the man was being truthful.

Logan glanced briefly at his men, almost as if giving some silent warning.

Near where Logan stood, Aaron noticed the blood drops he'd seen earlier. If the man looked down, he would see them. Aaron did his best to keep his reactions as normal as possible and his attention off the blood.

"This woman is responsible for the deaths of several members of a government agency. She's armed and dangerous. If you see her, call me immediately." Logan wrote his number on a card and held it out. Aaron scrubbed his hand hard along the lining of the jacket pocket in hopes of wiping the blood from his hand. "I realize you don't have phones in your houses, but I recall seeing a shared phone near the Amish businesses. Take the card." Logan's hard eyes pinned him in place.

Aaron grabbed the card and shoved his hand back into his pocket while Logan closely watched his reaction.

The hairs on the back of Aaron's neck stood up. Without a doubt, Logan wasn't who he claimed to be.

"I will be sure to call if I see her," Aaron assured him as Logan continued to watch.

All he wanted was these men and the danger they represented off his property immediately, before things turned ugly.

Logan turned to leave, glanced down at his feet and stopped. "What's this?" He kneeled close to the blood spots and directed the flashlight in his hand on them, then aimed it at Aaron. "That's fresh." He waited for an answer.

While Aaron hated being untruthful, he was certain these men were up to no good. "It's probably from an animal. There have been several bear sightings lately. Perhaps someone wounded the animal." The explanation sounded flimsy and Logan clearly didn't buy it.

"Where is she?" Logan demanded with a scowl. Aaron didn't answer. No matter what, he wouldn't give up Victoria to these men.

Logan rose quickly and came to within a few inches of Aaron's face. "I repeat, where is she?"

"I don't know who you're talking about."

"You're lying." Logan shoved past him. Before Aaron could stop the man, he yanked the door open and went inside. His men all but trampled Aaron as they followed.

The thought of what these men would do to Victoria if they found her was unimaginable. He hurried after Logan. In the middle of the workspace, his *sohn* stood alone and frightened, shielding his eyes from the flashlight beams.

Pushing past the men, Aaron moved to Caleb's side in a protective gesture. "You have no right to come in here. This is a private business."

Logan swung on him. "We do if you're harboring a fugitive." The feral words spewed out of his mouth. He glanced around the building with his eyes flashing in anger. "Search it. She's injured. She can't have gone far. Find her."

Aaron gathered his *sohn's* trembling body close. "It will be *oke*." But he had no idea if that were true. He couldn't imagine how difficult it would be for his *sohn* to watch Victoria being dragged off by these men. Or, worse, shot in cold blood. The thought of what Logan would do to him if he found out Aaron was hiding Victoria was terrifying.

Oh, Gott, *please put Your protective shield around her.* The silent prayer sped through his head while the men moved around his workroom. They disappeared into his office and returned empty-handed.

Logan came back a few minutes later with his people. "By hiding her you can get into a lot of trouble." The warning was meant to terrify, and it did.

Aaron squared his shoulders and did his best not to show it. "I told you I don't know this woman." That much was true. He suspected Victoria's life held many secrets few could understand.

Logan closed in. "If you're lying and I find out I'll be back. It won't go easy for you or your family." The man's nasty gaze landed on Caleb, who hid his face against his father's side.

With a quick nod to his companions, Logan stormed past, his men following, leaving the door wide open.

Aaron blew out a breath, relieved they were gone.

While Caleb clung to his father's side, Aaron went to the door and closed it. He moved as far away from the door as possible in case the men were close and listening.

"Where is she?" he whispered.

"In the woodpile." Caleb's voice shook so much the words were almost impossible to understand. The boy ran to the stacked pieces of used lumber and pulled several away. Victoria was curled up in a small burrow. And she wasn't moving. Had she survived those men only to die here in his workshop?

Aaron kneeled beside her and found a weak pulse.

He turned to Caleb. "Let's get her to the house right away." First, he had to be sure the men weren't out there waiting for them to make a foolish mistake. "Stay here with her for a second."

Aaron slipped outside. Daylight had broken. Logan's people had moved beyond the workshop and were heading toward Samuel's property. He went back inside. "Caleb, extinguish both lanterns. It's light enough outside that we don't need them to carry her out to the wagon."

While his *sohn* rushed to do as he asked, Aaron gently lifted the unconscious woman in his arms. He hesitated a second before stepping outside. She'd tucked her weapon behind her back in the waistband of her jeans. A woman who lived by the gun. He couldn't imagine such a life. He slipped it into his jacket pocket. Caleb hopped into the wagon and assisted his father.

"I will get the quilt so she can stay warm." Caleb scrambled across the seat to retrieve one of the many handmade quilts his grandmother had created through the years. He gave it to Aaron, who tucked it tight around Victoria. Why hadn't she woken?

Aaron climbed up onto the bench seat with Caleb and grabbed the reins with unsteady hands.

As they started for home, all he could think about was the woman lying so ill in the wagon's bed. He sensed she had no one in this world to fight for her. No matter what, he'd be her protector until she could stand on her own.

A glance back confirmed their leaving hadn't drawn the men's attention. Still, Logan's threat kept playing through his head.

"Why did they hurt her?" Caleb's simple question was impossible to answer. How did he explain the *Englisch* world to his *sohn* when he didn't understand it himself? The Amish ways were simple and lacking in the violence these men practiced.

"They claim she did something wrong." He watched the boy process what he said.

"Do you believe she did?" Caleb's innocent face turned up to him. He reminded Aaron so much of Irene. She saw the good in people, even when others didn't.

Aaron shook his head. "I do not." He had nothing to base this feeling on other than the panic he'd witnessed in Victoria's eyes and the lies he was convinced Logan had spun. Whatever she'd done in the past, he did not believe her guilty of the crimes Logan claimed.

In the east, the sky had turned pink. Morning had arrived in the mountains. The shape of his house silhouetted against the new day was a welcome sight. There were times—even though a year had passed—he still expected to see Irene standing on the front porch waiting for him as she had many times throughout their marriage. She'd been his rock—the one to get him through his *daed's* passing. And he'd let her down. He hadn't been there when she needed him. He'd been too busy trying to keep his family and the business from falling apart to see how truly ill his *fraa* had become. It was a regret he'd carry with him always.

Aaron pulled up close to the porch and jumped to the ground. "Caleb, could you open the door for me?"

The young boy hopped down and bounded up the steps while Aaron carefully lifted Victoria into his arms once more. As he carried her to the porch, he was shocked by how light she felt.

How long had she been running from these bad men? A life like that was not a life worth living. She was a pretty woman, despite the physical toll that had obvious effects on her. Though she was different in looks and in manners from Irene, Aaron found himself drawn to the woman in his arms. When she awoke, would she keep right on running?

He stepped across the threshold to be met by his *mamm'*s surprise.

"Was iss letz?" Mamm asked. She clasped a hand to her throat, a worried gesture he recognized from the past.

Explaining what was wrong with the little that he knew was hard, but he tried. "She's been shot. She needs our help."

His mother didn't hesitate. "Take her to my room." He followed her up the stairs. Through the years, watching his *mamm* and *daed* show kindness to those in need had inspired him to carry on in their manner.

Aaron brought Victoria over to the bed and laid her down. "I will go to the phone shanty and call Dr. Edmunds right away."

Victoria moaned softly as she came to. Her haunted green eyes snapped to his. They seemed to look right through him.

A compassion he hadn't felt in a long time rose inside him and he leaned down, seeking to comfort her. "You're safe here. This is my home. Try to rest. I'm going to fetch the doctor who attends to our community." Before he could move away, her hand snaked around his arm. The strength in her grasp was surprising.

"No. No doctor. It's too dangerous. They'll be expecting that move. They're probably watching this house right now." What she said alarmed him. Was it true, or delusions from an injured woman?

Aaron slowly removed her hand. "The wound could get infected."

She shook her head. "It's too risky."

He gave in for the moment. "All right. My *mamm* can tend to your leg." He held Victoria's gaze for a second longer before he nodded to his mother and crossed to where Caleb waited. He and his *sohn* left the room.

The thought of such deadly people watching his family chilled him to the bone. These men wouldn't give up simply because they hadn't found Victoria yet. They'd keep looking. Aaron had no doubt this wasn't the last he'd see of Logan and his people.

TWO

A woman dressed in Amish clothing entered Victoria's line of sight. Salt-and-pepper hair peeked out from beneath her *kapp*. She resembled her son in many ways, including the same intense blue eyes. The woman's familiar Amish clothing ripped her heart to shreds. Though the color of her dress was different, the similarities were enough to remind Victoria of her mother.

"I am Martha." The woman smiled kindly as she introduced herself. "Please lie back and let me take care of you." Her voice was gentle, but her hand firm as she eased Victoria back against the pillow. "I must cut away your pants so I can see the wound better." She waited for an answer that didn't come before she turned away. "I will be right back. I will need to heat some water to clean the wound."

A door opened. The silence of the room closed in around Victoria.

Mamm. Aaron had called Martha this. The

Pennsylvania Dutch word for *mother* was as familiar now as the last time she'd spoken it aloud. Victoria clenched her hands until the nails dug into her palms. She fought against the unwelcome emotions from the past. Chasing after ghosts was a weakness she couldn't afford if she wanted to live.

Her eyes darted around the small room, assessing it. The bed was made of full round logs, and she had no doubt it was crafted by someone in the family, probably Aaron himself. A matching log dresser stood against the opposite wall and a nightstand near the bed. A wall hanging at the foot of the bed read If a River Had No Rocks, It Would Have No Song. Victoria swallowed several times. Her mother once had a similar wall hanging in their small home.

When she'd first come to the West Kootenai area, Victoria had no idea how hard being back among the Amish would be, or how many unresolved feelings she hadn't dealt with through the years. She'd simply buried them deep down—her MO.

The door closed softly. Martha had returned. The noise of material being torn forced Victoria up on her elbows. Martha ripped her jeans free from above the bullet wound. Victoria stared at the gaping hole there. The bullet was too deep to be visible.

"It will be okay," Martha assured her. She poured hot water into a basin, then soaked a washcloth and carefully cleaned the injury. Deep grooves appeared on either side of Martha's mouth as she smiled down at Victoria, belying her concern. "You should let my son fetch Dr. Edmunds. I am not used to treating such injuries." Her attention fixed on Victoria's face.

The bullet wound wasn't serious, and the bleeding had stopped. "It'll be okay. Just do the best you can."

Martha narrowed her eyes and slowly nodded. "I have some medicine that will keep the wound from getting infected."

Victoria forced a smile. "Thank you for your kindness." When she found enough breathing room between herself and the men gunning for her, she'd rest. That would do a world of good for her injured body.

Martha returned to her work. When she'd finished cleaning the wound, she opened the drawer on the nightstand, brought out a jar and removed the lid. The medicine's pungent smell filled the air. Martha applied the salve liberally and covered the wound with a clean bandage. The leg felt much better already, thanks to Martha's care.

Victoria rose to a sitting position and tentatively swung her legs from the bed. Pain tore up her injured leg when she planted her foot on the floor.

"You must rest now." Martha placed a firm hand on Victoria's shoulder. "Don't try to move."

There wasn't a choice. Too much was at stake for her to stay here. "I'm okay. I appreciate what you and your son have done for me, but it's best that I get going. I've put you and your family in enough danger as it is."

Martha's frown deepened. "Nonsense. You are welcome here. I will get you some clean clothes to change into."

Before Victoria could respond, Martha stepped from the room once more.

This family had opened their home to her even knowing she was a hunted woman. The Amish ways would be considered strange to someone unaccustomed to such simple acceptance, but for Victoria, it was what she'd craved since she'd been forced to leave the Plain world.

You can't go back to that time. The person you were back then is dead and gone. The truth taunted her. She was no longer worthy enough to be called Amish.

Rising slowly, she tested the injured leg. It would slow her down a lot, but at least she was mobile again.

A window nearby reflected a burgeoning

new day. Victoria eased closer and peered out at the snow-covered world facing her. She'd almost forgotten how much she loved this country. The wide-open spaces created a feeling that the world and its cares could never intrude into this peacefulness.

But this wasn't her life anymore.

Footprints below headed from the chicken coop to the woods beyond. Someone had been out there recently. The family? She ducked away from the window. What if those weren't Aaron's or his son's tracks? Men could be watching the back of the house already.

Instinctively, she reached for the Glock only to realize it was missing. The last she remembered, she'd tucked it into the waistband of her jeans. She felt inside the pocket of her jeans and found her cell phone, but nothing more. Her gaze flew around the room. The Glock wasn't here.

The door opened. Martha came in carrying a dark blue dress, much like the one she was wearing.

She handed it to Victoria. "This belonged to Aaron's wife." A reminiscent smile creased her face. "Irenė was close to your size."

Was. Aaron's wife had died. Victoria was all too painfully acquainted with the crippling pain associated with losing someone you loved. She'd felt it every day since David's death.

"What happened to her?" she asked quietly.

Martha hesitated for a breath. "She passed away last year."

The Amish were a private people that chose to keep their troubles to themselves. Victoria understood having secrets. She possessed plenty herself, the biggest being her true identity.

She stroked the material of the dress. Faded memories of her mother came to mind. Even after she'd become so ill, she always had a smile for her daughter. She'd died too young—barely twenty-five when the pneumonia claimed her.

Martha's eyes narrowed. Victoria had a feeling they missed little.

She turned away. At times, it felt as if most of her life had been defined by death—first her mother's, then David's and her entire CIA unit's. Not to mention those she'd killed in the name of justice.

Find the evidence. It's our own people... David's final words were always close, teasing her with the unknown. For most of the past year since his death, she had no idea what to make of them...until two weeks ago, when things had changed drastically.

Discovering the key David had hidden inside his boot was a gift from God. Victoria had tracked it to a storage facility and found a single six-by-six-inch metal box that held several surveillance photos and one photo that appeared to be taken of some type of ledger. It was a single blurred image showing a page of grouped numbers. At the time, she'd thought that was it. The answer she'd desperately searched for was now within reach. Yet, so far, nothing made sense.

"Once you've changed, come to the kitchen and I will get you something to eat. A warm meal will do you a world of good." Martha squeezed her arm and crossed the room. With a final glance, she left.

More than anything, Victoria longed to linger here among these peaceful people and heal her wounded soul, yet each second she stayed, she put innocent lives in death's crosshairs.

She laid the dress on the bed and kicked off her shoes. Getting out of her torn and grimy clothes proved more difficult with her injured leg and sore limbs. She slowly peeled off the old clothes and slipped the dress over her head, then pinned the cape and apron onto the dress. She dropped the phone into the pocket of the apron.

The dress's midcalf length covered the bullet wound from view. Dressing Amish would provide a good disguise. The men wouldn't be looking for an Amish woman.

Victoria shoved her feet into her sneakers

once more and balled up her stained clothes. She'd destroy them as soon as possible. If the house was searched and the clothing found, they'd know Aaron aided her in escaping. She'd seen what these men were capable of doing to protect their crimes.

She crossed to the door while favoring her wounded leg. Running again was the last thing she wanted, but the only choice. Retrieving the proof was crucial. If these men found it before her...

Victoria stepped out into the hall and slowly descended the stairs. Each step was a reminder of her depleted strength. If forced into a show-down, she wouldn't be able to defend herself for long.

At the bottom of the stairs, she stopped and surveyed the living room and the beautiful pieces of handcrafted furniture there. Each one spoke of the talent of its creator. Were they all Aaron's creations?

The boy who had helped her was seated near the fire warming his hands. He smiled shyly when he spotted her and gave her a little wave, which she returned. She owed Caleb her life. She couldn't have gotten out of sight on her own.

Near the window, the boy's father stood watch, a frown deepening the grooves on his handsome face. He was troubled, and for good reason.

Several candles had been placed on the windowsill, a reminder that Christmas was close. A dozen or more handmade cards hung near the door—an Amish tradition. No doubt Martha's doing. That last Christmas with her mother struggled to be remembered. *Don't go there*, her head warned, yet the sight of the decorations sent her back in time, and bittersweet memories swirled through her thoughts like so much shifting sand.

The tiniest of breaths slipped past her lips, bringing Aaron's attention to her. His gaze swept over her Amish attire. Something flared briefly in his eyes—was gone before she could name it—yet a shiver sped through her body. Was he remembering the woman who'd once worn this dress? The one he'd lost.

"How are you feeling?" he asked. His husky voice carried in it the same strength she'd seen earlier. He was someone to trust…if only she could allow herself to trust anyone.

"Much better. Thank you for your hospitality, and for the use of the clothes." She touched the dress. "I'll be on my way now. I've inconvenienced your family enough."

This was the first time she'd seen him clearly. Broad-shouldered, he was one of the few men she'd ever encountered that she had to look up to. Dressed in dark blue broadfall trousers and black suspenders, his button-up shirt was a slightly lighter blue. The shirt's color brought out his eyes. His hair was flattened from wearing the hat, but it curled where it touched his collar. His beard was slightly darker than his hair and reached past his chin—a reminder that he'd once been married.

"That would not be wise." He motioned her away from his son's hearing. "There are men out front at the edge of the woods. They are searching near the house. I noticed them when I put the wagon away. Probably the same ones who shot you."

Shocked, she started for the window, but Aaron grabbed her arm before she could move away.

"What are you doing?" she asked with a flash of anger.

"Trying to keep you from making a mistake. Right now, they're simply searching. They don't know you are here. They might see you in the window. And if you try to run, they certainly will. The best thing to do is stay out of sight."

If only it was that easy. But if her instincts were correct, these men were part of the CIA, the same agency she'd once worked for. They wouldn't be happy with just searching the property.

"You don't understand. They'll come into the house one way or another. They won't let a little thing like a locked door or what's right or wrong stand in the way. And if they find me with you, they'll kill us all." His eyes widened and he flinched at her directness.

She'd been living on her own for far too long and had forgotten how to temper the impact of her words. "Look, right now, they don't really know you're involved." Victoria glanced out the window of the back door. If she could make it to the woods beyond the yard without being spotted, perhaps she could get away on foot.

"I need my weapon." Her gaze returned to Aaron's troubled expression.

He blinked several times. "I have it in my jacket pocket, but you are no match for so many, Victoria. You cannot go out there and risk taking them on by yourself."

While she agreed, staying wasn't an option, either. "I'll be okay. Please, let me go."

But he didn't. His hand still rested on her arm. "And where would you go? You're injured. There are many of them. One of you. Please, wait here. Let me help you."

Her eyebrows shot up. "No one can help me but me. I must go back to my cabin. There's information there that will explain why these men are coming after me. Hopefully, it will put them away for what they've done. Without it, I have nothing."

"You live near here?" Her admission came as a surprise to him, she noted.

Since the bombing that killed her entire CIA unit, Victoria's life had been turned upside down. Coming stateside, she'd almost died several times by a series of "accidents." She'd known then that the warning David had voiced before his death were true. So she'd quit the CIA, started using her former Amish surname from before she was adopted and disappeared. Yet with each new move, the men kept finding her and she had no idea how.

"Yes. I've rented a cabin at the base of the mountains. That's where I was when they found me this morning."

"I know the place. They'll be watching it, expecting you to return. You can't go back there," he insisted.

"I don't have a choice." Victoria told him about finding the metal box containing photos. She still couldn't believe she'd carried around the storage key for almost a year and didn't even know about it. For so long, she hadn't been able to bring herself to look at the clothing David had worn on that final mission.

"Who are these men?" he asked once she'd

finished. The expression of disbelief on his face told her how bizarre her claims sounded.

"I believe they are CIA agents." Speaking the truth out loud—even after she'd had time to accept it for herself—was hard. She told him about David's final words.

"I cannot imagine going to such extremes simply to cover up a crime." Aaron had the same reaction she'd had when David uttered those dying words. When she'd first voiced her concerns to Robert, he hadn't wanted to believe it, either. It was hard to imagine their own people could betray them in such a way.

She pinched the spot between her eyes where a migraine had taken up residence. Lack of sleep—and worry—was taking a toll. Her mind whirled with disjointed thoughts.

"I'll need to get rid of these clothes," she said when she remembered the soiled clothes in her hand. "If they find them…" Though she didn't finish, Aaron seemed to understand. He took the clothes from her and carried them to the wood-burning stove in the center of the room. He opened the glass door, then tossed them inside and waited until they caught before he returned.

"Perhaps you should borrow a prayer *kapp*, as well, to cover your hair." He glanced past her to where Martha stood in the middle of the kitchen.

"*Jah*, that's a *gut* idea. I will get one and fix your hair for you." She hastened upstairs and returned moments later with a prayer *kapp*. Soon, under Martha's skilled hands, Victoria's blond hair was secured in a bun and hidden from view.

Aaron narrowed his eyes as he surveyed her for several seconds. "To a stranger, you could pass as Amish." Regret hit her hard. She'd been one of them…once.

He returned to the window and parted the curtains.

Victoria slipped in behind him and out of sight. Nothing appeared as far as she could see. Yet her spine tingled an alarm. They were close. She could feel it.

The thought barely took hold before a figure stepped up onto the porch. Aaron dropped the curtain in his hand as the man knocked on the door and jiggled its handle. They both jumped away from the window.

Another knock—louder than the first one—sounded throughout the house. "Anyone inside? Open up."

Victoria's gaze locked with Aaron's. Each second ticked by in time with her heart.

Then the pounding was replaced with something of weight being slammed against the wood door. Just like at her cabin. They weren't even trying to play nice.

Caleb leaped to his feet. His troubled eyes beat a path to his father's. Aaron placed a finger to his lips to keep his son quiet and grabbed his jacket from its peg. He retrieved Victoria's Glock and handed it to her, then reached for a shotgun leaning close to the door.

"We have to get to the basement before they break down the door. Hurry," he whispered to his mother and son.

Victoria followed the family to the kitchen, where Aaron opened a door next to the stove and was met with absolute darkness. He retrieved a lantern from a nearby peg and lit it. The light illuminated a landing and a set of stairs.

From the front of the house, the men continued trying to gain entrance.

"Quickly." Aaron ushered her inside. She ran down the steps to the basement with Martha and Caleb almost right on top of her.

Aaron closed the door and followed them down into a basement cluttered with old furniture and boxes. Victoria looked around for some means of escape. There wasn't any.

"What now?" she asked while trying to curb her concern.

He pointed to another door almost hidden

by stored furniture. "The root cellar is through there."

At the front of the house, the door finally gave way. Multiple sets of footsteps stormed inside.

"Search the place!" the same man from before yelled.

Aaron opened the second door and waited for her to go inside. The room was tiny in size and stocked with canned goods. If the men tore apart the basement—and they would—they'd be trapped.

"We can't stay here. We'll be sitting ducks."

Aaron indicated a rear door that she'd overlooked. "That leads out to the side of the house. It's on the opposite end from the back door and away from the front. If we can make it to the woods without being spotted, we'll head to my parents' home. Help me move this hutch close to this door. Hopefully, it will disguise the entrance."

With his family secured inside, Aaron grabbed one side of the solid wood hutch. Victoria moved to the other. It was a struggle to shove the heavy piece of furniture in front of the door, but they managed, leaving enough room for them to slip inside.

Victoria hurried to the outer door and twisted the handle. It didn't give. Shoving the Glock into the pocket of her apron, she tried it again with the same result.

"It won't open." She faced Aaron and tried not to lose it.

"The door sticks sometimes." He grabbed the handle and threw his shoulder against it. The door didn't budge.

Movement upstairs grew louder. They were right outside the basement entrance.

"There's no sign of anyone in the house," another unidentified man said.

"Well, someone's been here recently. There's a lit fire and signs of a meal being prepared in the kitchen. And the family didn't just disappear," the less-than-patient voice barked. The same man who had spoken at her cabin earlier. "Check the basement. They could be hiding down there."

"We don't have much time," Victoria said and went back to work on the door. It took both of them shoving against the door to finally get it to budge. Aaron started through the opening, but she stopped him.

"Let me go first. They could have men stationed nearby expecting this move."

She could tell he didn't like the idea, but trying to protect his family was the least she could do.

Victoria drew her weapon and eased from

the root cellar. Snow piled up high on this side of the house, where there was little sunlight, which meant there would be no disguising their footprints. When the men found the exit, they'd see and come after them. Their only chance at surviving was if they could reach Aaron's parents' home without being spotted.

She closed the outside door as quietly as possible and hoped the hutch would allow enough cover to keep the men from discovering the root cellar. "Head for the trees, and whatever you do, don't stop."

Aaron didn't move. "Not without you." As she searched his handsome face, the truth was clear and easy to see. He was an honorable man.

"All right." Victoria heaved out a breath and gave in.

Though different from David in many ways, Aaron was a strong and valiant man. Like David, he wouldn't leave her behind. She prayed Aaron's honor wouldn't end up costing him his life…like David's had.

Aaron turned to his mother. "Stay close to me." The fear on *Mamm's* face was hard to witness. He grabbed his *sohn's* hand and felt the boy quaking. As he stepped from the protection of the house, all he could think about was keeping his family safe.

It took forever to cover the short distance between the house and woods. All the while Aaron kept expecting someone to jump out at them and open fire.

"Search the barn and the rest of the property," the man's voice Aaron recognized as Mike Logan shouted his irritation. He sounded as if he were standing on the back porch. "We missed her before. That can't happen again. They're hiding her somewhere. Find out where."

"What's the plan?" Victoria asked once they reached the trees. "Which way do we go?" She turned to Aaron and rubbed her injured leg.

"Straight ahead leads to my parents' home."

Victoria nodded. "You go first. I'll be right behind you."

Holding her gaze, Aaron understood what she wasn't saying. When the men came after them, there'd be a shoot-out. It was now only a matter of whether they escaped with their lives.

He gathered his *mamm* and *sohn* and started toward his parents' old house, where his brother Fletcher still lived. Thankfully, Fletcher wouldn't be home. He'd left well before sunrise to deliver a couple of rockers to the store in Eureka.

"I see movement up ahead!"

Aaron swung toward the man's voice.

"Hurry. Get out of sight. They're almost

here." Victoria grabbed his arm and urged him toward several large trees. Once he was behind them, she eased closer to the approaching men.

With his mother and *sohn* tucked out of sight, Aaron went after Victoria.

She held up two fingers. The meaning became clear. Two men were coming their way.

Aaron only used the shotgun for hunting food and warning off predators. The Amish were pacifists who did not believe in hurting others. Could he bring harm to another human to protect his family? He swallowed several times without finding a clear answer.

He held the weapon in his unsteady hand. A twig snapped close by. The first man slowly eased past their hiding spot. Victoria slipped up behind the unaware man and grabbed him in a choke hold before he could get his weapon in position or alert his partner. He fought to free himself like a wild animal. Aaron ran to assist, but it wasn't necessary. The unconscious man's full weight slumped against Victoria. Aaron grabbed his feet. Together, they carried him out of sight.

The second man—still some distance behind his partner—heard the commotion and opened fire in their direction. Aaron hit the ground. Without flinching, Victoria returned the man's shots. A scream sounded over the gunshots. She'd wounded the second man.

"The others will have heard. If we don't get out of sight now, they'll cut us off." She pulled Aaron to his feet and limped toward his mother and *sohn*.

Victoria grabbed his mother's hand and didn't slow down. Caleb seemed incapable of moving. He stared back at the wounded man with a look of terror on his face.

"Don't worry about him. He has people coming to assist. We have to go." Aaron snatched Caleb's hand and ran.

"How much farther?" Victoria asked once he and Caleb reached them.

"We are almost there." As if on cue, the house peeked through the trees. Even as an adult, seeing it had always given him a sense of coming home…until the day his *daed* passed. Since that time three years ago, it was difficult making this trip. After Irene's death, his mother had come to stay at his home to take care of the house and Caleb, though he suspected she missed her husband greatly and found it hard to stay in the house she'd shared with him for so many years.

They cleared the trees not a second too soon. What sounded like a half-dozen men tramped through the woods behind them. Once they found their partners, they'd know which direction to go. Staying at the house wasn't an option.

"Caleb, come with me to harness the buggy. Quickly." Aaron ran toward the family barn near the house. His *mamm* followed them inside while Victoria kept guard near the door. Working alongside his *sohn*, he had the mare in place behind the family's enclosed black buggy in no time.

"They're coming," Victoria warned.

Aaron assisted his mother up into the back of the buggy, where two bench seats facing each other were hidden from view. Victoria climbed up beside Caleb while Aaron shook the reins in his hand. The mare trotted forward.

"Caleb, get in the back with your grandmother and both of you get on the floor. Cover your heads," Victoria told them. She kept her attention on the flashlights bouncing through the woods nearby.

The boy clambered across the seat and sat on the floor next to his grandmother. She tugged him close.

The first group of men reached the clearing.

Aaron clicked his tongue. "Go, mare." The horse seemed to sense the urgency. She galloped forward at a quick pace.

"Get down!" Victoria yelled. A breath later,

the men opened fire. Aaron ducked as low as he could and still see to guide the horse.

Victoria quickly returned fire, forcing the men back among the trees. She kept them pinned down until the buggy had covered some distance. "Whatever you do, don't slow down."

Aaron kept the mare's pace steady and fast. "There's an old logging road up ahead. If we can make it there, it winds through the woods out of sight from the main road. Several trails veer off from it." He looked over at her.

She glanced behind them. "I don't see anyone coming, but then again, I had no idea they'd find my place so easily." She twisted in her seat to face him. "We need somewhere to get out of sight, and fast."

Aaron could think of only one place. "My brother Hunter's home is on the other side of the community. We should be safe enough there."

A frown creased her forehead. "As much as I hate bringing anyone else in on this, I don't think we have a choice."

Behind him, *Mamm* and Caleb reclaimed their seats. The quiet of the passing countryside was interrupted only by the mare clomping through thick snow.

Aaron reached inside his pocket and handed her a card. "One of the men at my workshop gave me this. He said is name was Mike Logan."

She took the card where Logan had scribbled his name and a phone number.

"He claimed to be a federal agent," Aaron said, and watched her reaction. "Logan said you were a fugitive."

She looked him in the eye. "Do you believe him?"

As he continued to study her, the answer he'd given his *sohn* was still the same. "No. I don't believe him."

Victoria's attention returned to the writing on the card. "I don't recognize his name." She glanced up at him. "What did he look like?"

Aaron did his best to describe Logan. "Tall. Stout. Dark eyes. He wore a cap so most of his hair was hidden, though I believe it was dark. He's probably in his forties."

She pulled in a breath and shook her head while her attention returned to the countryside as it passed by. Her eyes were alert, watchful. The weight of the world seemed to rest on her shoulders. She'd told him very little of what had happened to her, yet he could see the strain she was under. High cheekbones were sunken. She'd been shot, and yet it didn't slow her down. Victoria had suffered so much at the hands of the men who killed her partner. Would she pay the ultimate price with her life? Would they all?

THREE

Mike Logan. No matter how many times she repeated the name in her head, the answer was the same. She didn't recognize it.

These men coming after her were ruthless, with everything to lose. And if she didn't figure out what was really going on soon, she might not have the chance. Any evidence of the crimes they were trying to cover up would be destroyed, along with the lives of innocent people.

A glance behind her proved they weren't being followed so far. How much longer would that last?

Victoria focused on the facts that she knew. She'd been so careful not to use the burner phone unless necessary. The last call had been the previous day, when she'd updated Robert on what the storage facility contained. Each time she spoke to him, their conversation lasted only a handful of minutes before she'd turned off the phone. How did they manage to locate her? Was it possible they were using Robert's phone to track her? Most people who knew her at the CIA would be aware of her friendship with Robert. They'd expect her to reach out to him at some point.

"We are almost to Hunter's home." The edge in Aaron's tone assured her he was worried...with good cause. He leaned forward. The weight of their recent run-ins made him hunch his shoulders. Guilt tore her apart inside. She'd brought her troubles to him when he carried so much heartache already. Not long ago, he'd lost his wife. There was the boy to watch out for, as well as Aaron's mother. As soon as she was able, she'd leave them in peace and pray her mistakes wouldn't continue to stalk him and his family once she was gone.

He turned and caught her watching him. For a moment, their eyes held, and her heart flew into high speed at the tenderness in his eyes. She sucked in a breath. Aaron was a reminder of all the things from her past that were good... and all she'd once hoped for.

During the last year, every thought, memory and feeling had been centered on David and bringing the men who took his life to justice. There'd been no room in her world for anything else, and certainly not for the possibility of a future beyond this nightmare. She couldn't allow herself to have that hope.

She looked away, cleared her throat. Staying focused was imperative. There was work to be done and she wasn't about to let anything stand in the way of bringing down these ruthless men. The proof was there somewhere. She had to stay one step ahead to find it.

Aaron turned the buggy onto a snowy lane. Even though she'd existed off the grid since moving here two weeks earlier, keeping mostly to herself and rarely leaving the cabin, the beauty of the breathtaking Montana mountains and surrounding countryside was not lost on her. She hadn't been back to Montana since she'd left as that frightened little girl of five. If her life had taken a different turn, she could imagine living in a place like this, unencumbered by the past and the terrible things haunting her today.

A simple farmhouse appeared at the end of the lane. With snow on the rooftop and clinging to the surrounding trees, the view was picture-perfect—a Christmas postcard in the making. She imagined candles and wreaths on the kitchen table. Presents wrapped in gleaming paper placed near the hearth for Christmas Day. Dinner with the family gathered around the table to celebrate this special time of the year.

Aaron brought the mare to a halt in front of the house and jumped down. As soon as they arrived, a man opened the door and stepped outside. The family resemblance was unmistakable, though he appeared slightly younger than Aaron and didn't wear a beard, signaling he was unmarried.

The two brothers greeted each other with a hug. Their closeness was easy to see. Watching them together reminded Victoria of the things missing from her life.

While Aaron explained why they were there, the younger man shot Victoria a series of curious glances. She couldn't imagine what the Amish man must be thinking. Dangerous situations like the one she faced were far removed from their Plain way of life.

Caleb helped his grandmother out the back of the buggy while Victoria eased down off the bench seat, mindful of her injured leg.

As she approached, Aaron's gaze followed her, his expression as unreadable as the man himself. She'd give anything to know what he was thinking.

"This is Victoria Kauffman," he said, introducing her to his brother.

"Hunter Shetler." The younger man shook her hand. Victoria couldn't think of anything to say beyond hello. Living with only herself for company had taken away her ability to make small talk, and the exhaustion of the past year often affected her thinking.

"We should get the buggy out of sight to be safe." Aaron swung to his son. "Caleb, can you take the mare into the barn and unharness her?"

"*Jah*, I can do it." The boy eagerly did as his father requested. It was easy to see Caleb adored Aaron.

"Fletcher is delivering furniture to the store in Eureka today," Aaron told his brother. "Those men could still be waiting for him when he returns home."

Hunter nodded. "I can saddle the horse and ride to the phone shanty. I'll leave a message for Fletcher at the store to come here."

"*Denki*, Hunter." Aaron faced Victoria. "Let's go inside. I don't believe we were followed, but we cannot afford to be too careful."

Martha went ahead of them.

"You should sit for a while," Aaron urged when he noticed her favoring her leg.

Without answering, Victoria eased into one of the chairs near the inviting fireplace and stretched her leg out in front of her. She could sit here forever just watching the fire.

Caleb came inside and closed the door. "*Onkel* Hunter has left."

Aaron nodded. "*Gut*. Hopefully, the message

will reach Fletcher before he heads for home." Yet the worried frown he wore didn't disappear.

Victoria certainly understood. There was reason to be alarmed about the missing brother. They'd have people stationed near Aaron's home as well as Fletcher's, in case she returned.

"I will make us something to eat. I think we could all use a warm meal after what we've been through." Martha motioned for her grandson to come with her.

When the room grew quiet, Aaron claimed the chair beside Victoria. "How are you holding up?" The concern on his face was all for her and so undeserved. If only he knew who she really was. The dreadful things she'd done. Things that went against what the Amish believed. Beliefs her mother had held sacred.

She forced a smile. "I'm okay." Not the truth, but she'd gotten used to ignoring pain and hiding her true feelings. Aaron glanced at her subconscious action of rubbing her leg and she stopped. "I guess it does hurt some."

"You'll be safe here. Perhaps you should get some rest. You will feel better."

Victoria shook her head. If she ever let herself fall asleep, she'd be out for days, and she couldn't afford the luxury. Too much was at stake.

"I can't rest until I have the evidence. I have

to go back, Aaron. It's all I have to link these men to David's death."

He leaned closer and held her gaze. "David was your partner?"

She wanted to be honest with him, but speaking about David was hard even now. "He was more than my partner. I loved him. Wanted to spend the rest of my life with him." Victoria stopped and pulled in a calming breath. "I watched him die and promised I'd bring the people responsible to justice. I won't let him down."

Something akin to admiration flashed in Aaron's eyes. "I understand your loyalty, but won't they be expecting you to return to your home?"

Without a doubt. "It doesn't matter, I don't have a choice." Even though her leg would slow her down somewhat, Victoria couldn't ask him to risk anything more. He'd given enough. "If I could borrow your mare for a little while, I'll go to the cabin, get what I need and bring the horse back. Then, I'll leave your family in peace."

She rose and started for the door, but Aaron clasped her hand before she could move away. The calluses on his palm spoke of someone who worked hard with his hands. The exquisite pieces of furniture in his home proved he was a talented artist in his own right.

"You cannot do this by yourself. It's too much. I will go with you."

She dismissed the idea immediately. "No. I've put you and your family in enough danger as it is. You could die, Aaron." The truth had to be stated.

"I can take care of myself." The strong set of his jaw proved she'd have a fight on her hands if she disagreed. With his eyes fixed on her face, he waited for her response.

"All right," she murmured at last. Part of her wanted to insist he stay behind. The other was grateful she wasn't fighting this battle by herself.

Aaron slowly smiled and she couldn't look away. She had a feeling he didn't smile much, and it made him seem almost lighthearted.

"*Gut*, but first we wait for Hunter to return so he can protect my family if those men should come here."

"Of course." The last thing she wanted was for something to happen to Aaron's people.

Settling back in her chair, Victoria closed her eyes, content to simply sit quietly beside this courageous man and lean on his strength for a moment.

Something delicious-smelling came from the kitchen. She hadn't thought the canned soup she'd heated up the night before would be her last meal. Each time she ate it, she thought of David. That final mission. The meager rations they'd shared with the other members of their team. Before…

Soon, the sounds around her faded and she was back in Afghanistan. She'd relived those final hours dozens of times, the outcome always the same. They were there to meet with a man who had information on the massive amounts of heroin being smuggled from the country. Trevor Hawk, the mission's commander, had hoped to turn him into an asset. Before the meeting, Victoria couldn't dispel the feeling something was wrong. David had been on edge. Jumpy. She thought it was all because of what lay ahead of them. If only she'd asked the questions then she wanted to now.

Even today, she could still feel the eerie silence that preceded the explosion. She and David, the last ones in, had escaped most of the blast that gutted the inside of the building and killed their entire unit. David tried to get her out of the line of fire, but there were snipers waiting to finish the job. Though wounded, he'd fought his way to a safe location. She hadn't realized how seriously injured he was until it was too late. They'd both been flown to the same hospital in Afghanistan. She'd been at his bedside when he breathed his last breath. But not before he whispered those chilling words.

Find the evidence. It's our own people…

Somewhere in the house a door opened. Victoria fought her way back to the present. Her eyes snapped open. She'd let down her guard for a second—something she couldn't afford to do.

Aaron glanced her way. "It's only my brother coming inside." He stood and headed toward the door as Hunter entered. The tension on Hunter's face told her something had happened.

She rose and went over to the brothers. "What's wrong?"

Hunter removed his hat and coat and hung them up. "There are several *Englisch* men hanging around town. They watched me the entire time I used the phone." Hunter's gaze skipped to his brother. "I don't think they followed me, but I can't be sure."

How many armed men had they sent to take her down?

"Victoria, these men will not stop until they capture you or worse. Let me get the sheriff."

Going to law enforcement wasn't an option. The only person she trusted was Robert. If she failed to retrieve the evidence, she would have no choice but to ask for his help. Robert had been a good friend to both her and David, and she knew he would do everything in his power to assist.

"I can't. These men work for the same agency

I did. They can convince the sheriff they're telling the truth. It's too risky."

She struggled to come up with a workable solution without involving Aaron. Her heart urged her to leave before her war became his. With the Amish clothing, it was possible she might be able to make it back to the cabin undetected. Once there, she could find out how many men were watching her place and perhaps create a diversion that would allow her to get in and out of the cabin quickly.

"No, Victoria." Aaron's husky voice intruded almost as if he'd read her thoughts.

"Aaron…" She had to make him understand. "I'm grateful for what you've done, but I can handle it from here."

"That's not going to happen," he insisted.

She'd been fighting so long for the truth. Existing in secrecy. Living without hope of a future. More than anything, she wanted to move beyond this nightmare and live again. One thing stood in her way—David's death. She wouldn't let it go unsolved. The answers were there, she was positive of it. She just had to stay alive long enough to pull them out.

Horses' hooves clomping down the lane near the house pulled Aaron's attention away from the task of harnessing the buggy.

A wagon came into view, and his brother Fletcher was a welcome sight.

Since their *daed's* passing, Aaron and his middle brother, Fletcher, had followed in their father's footsteps of working the wood milled from the nearby wilderness by Hunter. The furniture they created was sold all around the state.

It had broken his *daed's* heart when Aaron's brother Mason left the Amish faith behind and became a US Marshal. The disagreement between Mason and their brother Eli had caused a rift in the family. Eli and his wife had moved away to Libby. Though the family hadn't seen either brother since Irene's funeral, their *mamm* never gave up hope that her sons would return to West Kootenai one day and join the family. Aaron wasn't nearly as convinced.

"There's Fletcher." Hunter glanced up from tightening the harness strap. When Aaron had first told his brother what he and Victoria had planned, Hunter insisted he should go with them. He'd not been pleased when Aaron refused, but Aaron couldn't involve his brother in this dangerous endeavor.

There was no doubt in his mind that the men coming after Victoria would be watching her cabin. They'd face armed men intent on taking her life. The thought of bringing harm to someone went against beliefs instilled in him since childhood. Yet he was all Victoria had, and he wouldn't let her down.

"Whoa, horses." Fletcher brought the team to a halt and hopped down. He came toward them with a purposeful stride.

"Glad you made it, brother." Aaron gave Fletcher a heartfelt hug. While he had agreed to aid Victoria and was determined to keep her alive, he didn't want his family involved in this threat—they'd all suffered enough.

Fletcher tipped back his hat, a serious expression hovering on his face. "I am grateful to be here in one piece. There are a lot of *Englischers* running around the community, for sure."

Aaron told Fletcher about what was happening with Victoria and his plans to help her retrieve the evidence box. He'd hoped the men would eventually give up and move on from the area, but judging by the amount of people around the community, they weren't showing any signs of it. His fear of what could lie ahead of them continued to grow.

"It's not wise for you and this woman to go alone, *bruder*." Fletcher's advice mirrored his younger brother's. "Take one of us with you."

He couldn't put them at risk when he wasn't sure how he would stand up to the challenges they might face. He was a peaceful man who had never lifted a hand in anger. Could he bring himself to possibly harm another person to protect Victoria?

Aaron shook his head. "The fewer people involved, the better. You are both needed here in case they show up. To protect *Mamm* and Caleb."

Once the buggy was ready for travel, Aaron led the mare outside the barn.

"Watch yourself," Fletcher warned. "There are many of them. It will be just you and the woman."

"I will." There were many things Aaron wanted to tell his brothers. "If I don't come back..." He couldn't bring himself to say the rest. His *sohn's* precious face appeared in his mind. Caleb had lost one parent. Was Aaron risking leaving the boy without either by giving assistance to a woman he hardly knew? Yet the lost look he'd seen on Victoria's face wouldn't allow him to do anything else.

"It will be *oke, bruder*," Hunter assured him. "We know what to do if you don't come back, but you should not think like that. It's in *Gott's* hands. Trust Him."

Aaron forced a smile for his brothers and glanced up at the home Hunter built five years earlier with his family and community. Hunter's bright plans had been destroyed by a tragic death. Had that been *Gott's* plan? Had Irene's death?

"They were not His fault," Hunter said, almost as if he'd read Aaron's angry thoughts.

But *Gott* hadn't done anything to help, even when Aaron's foolish pride had prevented him from seeing how ill his beloved wife truly was.

He and his brothers climbed up onto the seat and Aaron took up the reins. As they neared the house, Victoria stepped out onto the porch. Aaron couldn't take his eyes off her. She was nothing like Irene, yet she possessed the same type of courage he'd seen in his wife many times. Irene had battled ovarian cancer until her last breath. She'd made him promise not to live in sorrow for too long.

When he thought about those last moments with his wife, the guilt threatened to pull him under. He'd been so caught up with taking control of the business after his *daed's* passing that he hadn't realized how truly sick Irene had been. After he'd finally slowed down long enough to see beyond the happy face she wore for him, he'd rushed her to the hospital. But it was too late. She'd lived only a matter of days, and he'd blamed himself for her death ever since. He'd done everything in his power to do what Irene asked of him. But to not live in sorrow? How was that possible when each day he missed her more than ever?

An unsteady breath escaped his lips. Living in the past served no purpose. He had Caleb and his work. He would find happiness in them.

"I have my rifle in the wagon," Fletcher said. "I will get it for added protection." Both brothers hopped down and Fletcher hustled away.

Would it be enough? Though at times his faith was weak, now, more than ever, he needed *Gott's* strength.

"Please, *Gott*, I ask for Your protection over both of us," he whispered under his breath and jumped to the ground to assist Victoria.

When he held out his hand, she stared at it for the longest time. Victoria seemed unaccustomed to accepting anyone's help. From the things she'd told him, he gathered she'd lived on her own for a while. He had his *sohn*, his brothers and his *mamm*. They'd been his support after losing Irene. Facing such a tragedy alone, as Victoria had with her friend's passing, was unimaginable for Aaron. It made him want to support her all the more because she needed someone on her side.

Her soulful eyes grabbed onto his, pulling him into the storm raging there. She awakened feelings inside him that he thought were dead and gone, and just as unwelcome as the danger he would face with her.

She swallowed several times, then slipped her hand into his. Inches separated them. A half dozen or more freckles were sprinkled across the bridge of her nose. Her green eyes appeared huge against her pale skin. The smell of the outdoors—the wood fire—clung to her.

Victoria dragged in a breath, untangled her gaze from his and climbed up onto the seat.

Before Aaron got on board, Fletcher returned with the rifle and extra shells.

"Denki." He gratefully accepted the weapon and bullets and tucked them behind the seat. "I pray I don't have to use them."

Fletcher pulled him aside. The frown on his younger brother's face confirmed Fletcher's worry. "Be careful, brother. These men…" He chose his words carefully. "Their purpose for being here is bad. They do not believe like we do."

His brother's concerns were understandable. Aaron shared them all. "I will be careful. Keep a close watch around here. Take care of *Mamm* and Caleb."

Aaron turned back to the buggy, where Victoria waited, the biting wind blowing the cloak his *mamm* had given her for warmth. They'd be battling the cold the entire way. As much as he wanted to use the family's enclosed buggy because it allowed for more protection from the elements, it would be recognized. He couldn't take that risk.

Hoisting himself onto the buggy step, he swung up beside Victoria. The knot in his stomach tightened with the possibility of what might be waiting at her cabin.

The bitterly cold afternoon brought gray clouds that obscured the mountains. Snow threatened. He prayed the weather moving in would hold off a little while longer.

Aaron always carried along a couple of blankets for added protection against the elements. He reached behind the seat, grabbed one and placed it over Victoria's lap, then took up the reins. The mare responded immediately. He waved to his brothers as the mare trotted down the familiar path.

To be safe, he decided against following a direct route. It would take longer to reach the cabin, but by using the less-traveled back roads, he hoped to keep them out of sight.

As soon as they left Hunter's property, Victoria leaned forward, her body tense. She was on alert. Her eyes scanned the trees that lined the road as if she expected trouble soon.

"We'll take one of the older logging trails. It will allow us to bypass the main road in case they are watching it. Once we reach the wilderness near your cabin, we'll find a spot to leave the buggy and walk in." They'd have to be quick to get in and out without being spotted.

When she didn't respond, Aaron looked her way. A frown bunched her eyebrows together, confirming she was concerned. Her silver-blond hair peeked out from beneath the prayer *kapp*. She clutched his *mamm's* cloak tight around her slender body. He couldn't imagine the terrible things she'd seen while working with the CIA, but they'd left themselves imprinted on her face. He wondered if there would be a time in her future when she no longer wore those scars.

She slowly faced him and smiled. "Thank you. For not leaving me at the mercy of those men. You've sacrificed a lot to protect me. I realize violence isn't part of your faith, but I'm grateful for your help."

A curious statement. How did she know about the Amish beliefs? Most people had preconceived notions about their way of life, but few truly understood.

He skimmed her face. Though she'd been through so much, she was one of the strongest people he'd ever met. She'd survived an attack meant to kill her, had been running from threats for a year and had almost died today when the men found her in the cabin.

But, like him, she had scars that were not physical.

"You are welcome." He couldn't explain why he clasped her hand, but he did. She stared at their joined hands for the longest time before she gently pulled hers free. He suspected she wasn't used to having any form of human contact. She'd lived a very isolated life. It made him sad to think about her alone.

When they reached the logging road without running in to anyone, Aaron relaxed somewhat. The silence of the countryside he loved settled around them. Nothing could be heard but the noise of the horse plodding down the road. Occasionally, the mare snorted, sending a white puff of breath wafting in front, her ears pricked forward at some sound from the woods.

Aaron's thoughts wandered back to the woman at his side. There was plenty he did not know about her. Plenty he should.

The wilderness bordering the road spread to the right of them. So far, the trip had proven uneventful. He prayed it stayed that way.

After they'd traveled a little ways, he realized they wouldn't be able to take the buggy much farther. The dense trees around the cabin she'd rented made it almost impossible to get there except by foot. "How did you find the cabin in the first place?" He couldn't imagine getting a car in there.

"I have a four-wheel-drive vehicle. A Jeep. It's made for getting into tight spaces. Unfortunately, there wasn't time to get to it before I had to leave. We're getting close." She pointed up ahead. "The cabin trail is coming up soon, but we can't afford to take it. They'll be watching the trail."

Aaron knew the path she spoke of. He pulled back on the reins and the mare slowed while he kept his attention on the trees lining the road, looking for easy access into the woods.

Over the noise of the horse's hooves, another far more alarming sound from behind grabbed his attention. "Someone's coming."

Victoria whipped around. "I don't see the car yet, but they sound close. We have to get out of sight before they get here."

Aaron urged the mare to the left. The buggy's wheels sank into the deep snow, making it harder to gain traction. The horse struggled under the added burden, but stumbled up the embankment and into the trees.

Once they were out of sight, Aaron leaned forward enough to see the road. A car slowly passed.

He blew out a breath and turned to say something to Victoria. She wasn't looking at him—she was staring at the road.

"They're coming back."

He turned in time to see the car back up. "They saw our tracks." If the men ventured into the woods, they'd know he and Victoria were here. There was no way to hide the horse and buggy.

Aaron climbed down and Victoria jumped to the ground beside him. He grabbed his shotgun from behind the seat and handed Victoria the rifle and extra shells. She stuffed the shells into her apron pocket and checked the bullets in her Glock.

"Ready?" she asked, and he managed a nod. Was he really?

Victoria headed into the snowy woods, her feet sinking into the thick snow gathered there. They'd brought an extra weapon for protection, but he hadn't thought to bring heavy boots for them both.

The denseness of the trees blocked most of the sky from view. It was almost twilight and hard to see too far in front of them. The snow was up to their knees as they trudged along. It wasn't long before they were both out of breath.

Two car doors slammed shut on the road. Victoria placed her hand on Aaron's arm to get his attention. "There's no way we can outrun them," she whispered. "And it won't be long before they realize we're in here somewhere. I'm going to circle around behind and see if I can take them by surprise." She pointed to her left. "Wait here and stay out of sight."

Aaron didn't like the idea one bit. She'd be putting herself in danger with a good chance he might not be able to get to her in time to help.

"Don't worry. I'll be okay." She started off without waiting for his response. It amazed him how quietly she moved through the woods, but this was what she'd once done for a living.

"Someone's here." From his hiding spot, Aaron was able to see the man who spoke. He'd been with the group outside Aaron's workshop earlier that morning. The man was armed and had his weapon drawn and ready. "It's one of those Amish buggies."

"Why would they park in the woods?" a second guy asked. "Something's off. They have to be in here somewhere."

The man near the buggy moved toward the place where Aaron was hiding. Aaron ducked behind the tree. He could no longer see anything. As he listened, muffled footsteps came closer. By the noise of his breathing, it sounded as if the man was standing right next to the tree. Where was Victoria?

The man entered his line of sight once more. If he looked to his right, he'd spot Aaron.

Aaron hugged the tree and prayed he wouldn't be noticed.

The man muttered something under his breath before calling to his partner. "I don't see anyone here. What about you?"

Silence followed.

"Did you hear me?"

The sound of a scuffle came from the direction where Victoria had disappeared.

Aaron edged away from his hiding spot enough to see what was taking place. Victoria was engaged in a hand-to-hand struggle with the second man, who had a good fifty pounds on her. Aaron ran from his cover without thinking, and he was spotted immediately.

"That's far enough." The deadly edge in the man's tone stopped him in his tracks. "Drop that weapon and get your hands up." Aaron slowly faced him. Giving up his shotgun would leave him defenseless. It wasn't an option. He had to find a way to get to Victoria. She was in a life-and-death struggle with her attacker. Aaron wasn't sure how much longer she could hold off the man.

She took a blow that sent her reeling backward to the ground. Before Victoria could get up, the man grabbed her around the neck.

"Victoria!" Aaron made a run for her again, and the man standing guard fired off a warning shot, missing Aaron's head by inches as he ducked. He'd have to find a way to get past this guy's gun.

Momentarily distracted, Victoria's attacker jerked toward the sound. She grabbed the rifle from where she'd dropped it and slammed it against his head. He went down hard.

Panicked, the man near Aaron leveled his weapon at Victoria. He had her in his sights, ready to fire.

Aaron rammed into the man full force, and he stumbled backward, somehow keeping his legs under him.

Fighting with a fury he didn't know he possessed, Aaron wrestled for control of the weapon, but the man was strong.

As a *kinna*, he and his brothers had horsed around plenty, but all in good fun. This man was seriously trying to end Aaron's life. The concept went against everything he believed in.

Aaron was shoved hard. Before he had time to right himself, the weapon was inches from his face. A look of triumph quickly shifted to surprise when Victoria grabbed the man from behind and wrapped her arm around his throat. She worked with the skill of someone who had been in this position many times before.

"Look out!" she shouted when the man's finger connected with the trigger. Aaron hit the ground as the weapon discharged. The bullet ripped through his jacket and shirt and grazed his upper arm before it lodged in a nearby tree.

The man thrashed around violently, trying to free himself from Victoria's grip. Aaron bolted toward the two. He wrestled the gun from the man's clutches and put it in his pocket. After several failed attempts to free himself, he finally went limp. His body weight forced Victoria to the ground beneath him.

Aaron yanked the unconscious man off her, and Victoria rose quickly. She stared down at her attacker while dragging in several winded breaths.

"Help me get these two to the car and out of sight. Their people will have heard the gunshots. We won't have much time." She clutched the man's feet. "Can you grab his arms?"

Together, they lifted the man and started for the car. Sweat formed on his forehead as they stumbled through the deep snow.

Victoria dropped the man's legs. "Wait here." She moved to the driver's side, pulled the keys from the ignition and dropped them into her apron pocket.

After hitting the trunk's release, she returned. "Let's get them both inside the trunk. If they manage to get out, they won't be able to come after us without the keys. Their buddies will be here soon enough to rescue them." She grabbed hold of the unconscious man's legs once more and they heaved him into the trunk.

"Quick, we need to get the other man out of sight." As they headed to the remaining man, her breathing was labored. Having to disable two men had taken its toll. The limp in her injured leg was more pronounced, but she didn't quit.

Once both men were out of sight, Victoria closed the trunk and grabbed the remaining weapon. "Let's get out of here before others arrive."

They headed back to the buggy. With all the gunfire, the mare was on edge. Aaron did his best to calm the animal, but she pawed at the ground and slung her head in a panic.

"You're *oke*." He stroked the horse's side, then her head. "Settle down, mare. It's okay." The horse whinnied nervously with her eyes wild.

They were running out of time, but if he tried to force the animal to go when she was in a state of shock, he couldn't be sure of the outcome.

He continued to pet the horse's muzzle until she calmed enough for him to climb onto the buggy beside Victoria.

Aaron clicked his tongue and gently jostled the reins. The mare lurched forward and nickered loudly before she slowly eased past the car.

On the road, Aaron urged the horse into a faster pace. His fears rose. He had no idea what might be waiting for them at the cabin.

"I think we should turn back." He faced her and tried to get his point across. "They will know we're coming and will be waiting for us. We should return to Hunter's place for now. We can come back later."

She rejected the idea immediately. "I don't have that choice, Aaron. I have to keep going. If I lose the information David left me, I have nothing. I might never find out what happened to him, and these men will keep coming. Eventually, they'll find me." He didn't have to ask what would happen then. She paused for a breath. "But maybe you should go back. This is my fight, not yours," she said when he would have argued. "I shouldn't have put you in the middle of it."

He thought about his *sohn* and his promise to Irene not to let anything bad happen to him. Losing his father would devastate Caleb. But he couldn't let Victoria face those men by herself.

"I'm not turning back. We do this together." He saw all her misgivings and sought to put them to rest. "I'm going, Victoria. It is settled."

She slowly nodded. "Okay." She squeezed his arm and smiled in a way that transformed her face. He could almost imagine what she'd look like without the threat of death hanging over her head.

For the first time, she noticed the blood on his jacket and her smile disappeared. "You're bleeding. You were hit." She leaned in close to examine the damage, her fingers gentle against his skin. "It doesn't appear too bad. Are you in pain?"

She searched his face. She was worried about him. This woman who had suffered so much was worried about him.

He cleared his throat. "No, it's nothing more than a scratch."

Her pretty face slowly relaxed and she bit her bottom lip, drawing his attention to her mouth. As he watched her, his breathing grew heavy, as if he'd run a mile, and it had nothing to do with what they'd survived back there. It was all because of Victoria. She was responsible for creating feelings in him that he couldn't accept.

She clasped her hands together in her lap. "When I first came to the cabin, I scouted the area." This caught him by surprise, and she saw it. "I wanted to make sure I had the lay of the land in case something like this happened. There's a spot up ahead where you can hide the buggy. It will take us longer to reach the cabin, but hopefully, they won't be expecting us to come in from this direction."

He couldn't take his eyes off her. Aaron had never met someone so brave in all his life. How could he not do everything in his power to see her through this? But if it came to the choice of taking another's life to save his own or Victoria's, could he? He wasn't sure.

"I'm grateful to you, Aaron." The sincerity in her eyes burrowed into his heart. There was something special about this woman who had endured so much.

Getting words out was hard, but he tried. "I will do whatever you need me to in order to bring these men to justice. For David's sake. And yours."

Tears appeared in her eyes and she struggled to hold them back. This woman who had taken down four armed men had a softer side.

Aaron brushed a calloused hand across her soft cheek. Her eyes widened at his gentle touch. The tender moment between them took him by surprise as much as it did her. His conscience was quick to remind him of all his failures. He'd failed Irene. What if he did the same to Victoria? What if he let her die?

The possibility made him feel inadequate. His hand dropped. He focused on the road while wishing so many things could be different. He and Victoria shared a common bond. Both had lost someone they loved, yet his heart was so encased in guilt, he couldn't imagine a time when he would be free enough to let someone else in.

He hadn't cherished enough the gift of love *Gott* had once given him. He'd let other things become too important. *Gott* wouldn't give someone like him the opportunity to make that mistake again.

FOUR

She turned to the trees lining the road, searching for the safest place to leave the buggy—or so she told herself. The truth was far more disturbing. Despite all her efforts to build a wall around her feelings, Aaron had gotten through. Maybe because he reminded her of the things she'd once believed possible.

As a little girl, her mother would tell her stories about the strong and handsome man who won her heart. Victoria's father. He'd died in a farming accident when Victoria was just a toddler.

Back then, she'd wanted her life to be exactly like her mother's. Victoria had no idea how much her world would change in only a short period of time.

Let it go... Dwelling on the past served no purpose. There were plenty of troubles for today.

Aaron's husky voice overpowered the voices of doubt in her head. She shifted to him with her eyebrows raised because she hadn't really been paying attention.

"I'm sorry?"

"The place you scouted out to leave the buggy. Is it close?"

"Oh." She nodded and wrestled with emotions that had no place in the here and now. Not if she wanted to stay alive. "Yes. It's not far from here on the right side of the road." She leaned forward and watched the passing scenery while her heart slowly steadied.

"There." She pointed to a spot that would be easy enough for Aaron to lead the horse out of sight.

He clicked his tongue and the mare climbed the gentle slope to the woods. Aaron didn't look her way. Had he seen the things she couldn't hide? The wishes of her heart?

She pushed them down deep. No matter what, she couldn't change the outcome of her life now. Keeping herself and Aaron alive was critical.

Under Aaron's expert care, the mare slowly stopped. The animal was still spooked after the earlier attack. Not that Victoria could blame it. She was rattled, as well.

Victoria jumped down and grabbed a pine branch. "Help me cover our tracks." She headed out to the road, and Aaron followed her lead.

They worked quickly to cover the tracks.

Once they'd finished, she surveyed their work. "That should keep them from seeing which way we've gone. Hopefully, they'll think we kept going." But her gut told her once those two were discovered in the trunk, the enemy would fan out through the woods and double the coverage on her cabin. Their window to claim the proof she'd left there was quickly closing.

Her injured leg throbbed painfully and slowed her down considerably. The cabin was a good quarter mile away. The temperature in the woods had dipped well below freezing. She clutched the cloak tight for protection against the cold. Her thick stockings were soaked from the knee down. Neither she nor Aaron would be able to stand the bitter temperatures for long.

A frightened bird flapped its wings nearby and flew away. Victoria whirled toward the sound with her weapon drawn. Her worst nightmare was that David's evidence had been found already. She'd only begun to study the photos, but she had no real idea what he was trying to tell her.

"You should slow down. It will keep you from being so winded."

She stopped and faced him, ready to disagree, but he was right. She managed a smile. "There's no telling what we'll find once we reach the cabin. We'll need all our strength."

Aaron started walking again. He never once wavered, even knowing the danger they might be heading into.

While her body was on full alert, her mind sifted through the things she knew so far.

These men all appeared highly trained, which gave credence to David's belief that his own team had betrayed him. The way they pursued her was relentless. They'd found every single one of her hiding places, despite Victoria taking extreme precautions. If these men were truly CIA, as she believed, they'd have unlimited resources at their fingertips, and they had nothing to lose. Which meant they wouldn't stop until she was either dead, or had exposed their secrets.

She swung to face Aaron. "Did you recognize any of the men back there?"

He glanced her way. "*Jah*. The one holding me at gunpoint was at the building this morning along with a man named Logan. I recognized Logan's voice at my house earlier. He's clearly the one in charge."

Her eyes widened. She'd heard the man's voice Aaron spoke of and was inclined to agree with him. The man called Logan had been calling the shots at her cabin earlier.

According to Aaron, there were four men at his shop. She'd counted at least half a dozen at his house. How many more were out there looking for her, and, more importantly, why? What was in the evidence that had someone from the CIA so worried?

She suddenly noticed Aaron wasn't at her side—he had stopped. She looked back and found him studying the ground.

"What is it?" she asked and went over to where he stood.

Dozens of footprints covered the ground. Someone had been in the woods recently. The recent snow flurries hadn't had time to disguise the tracks. This was the opposite direction from which she'd left the cabin earlier that morning. Without a doubt, she believed the men had gone back there and had probably tossed the place in search of what she'd found at the storage facility. When they came up empty, they'd fanned out through the woods, expecting her to have hidden it in a safe location away from the house.

A chill slipped between her shoulders. Those men could be anywhere. If the men engaged her in another shoot-out, this was her battle to fight. Aaron was an innocent bystander who had gone out of his way to be there for her. She couldn't let him sacrifice his life for her war.

"Why don't you hang back here? I'll make better time alone. Let me go in and get the evidence—"

He stopped her right away. "No, Victoria." He took her hands in his. "I have seen what these men are capable of. I'm coming with you."

Aaron possessed a valor that couldn't be taught. It was ingrained in a person's very being. David had been the same way.

His eyes, filled with a compassion she didn't deserve, searched her face. "What these men did to you and to your friend is hard for someone like me to understand, but I know it is wrong. Why would they choose to harm one of their own?"

"I wish I knew," she said with a frustrated sigh. "So far, I don't understand anything about the photos David took." She began walking again and Aaron fell into step beside her. "But I know they're important because of the steps he went to ensure they weren't found by the wrong person." She told him about the dozens of storage facilities around David's home she'd checked.

"How did you find the right one?" She noticed the way he kept checking their surroundings. They were both on pins and needles, expecting the bad guys to attack at any moment.

"I searched them all," she said with a smile. "I finally found the right unit registered under David's alias. When I opened it, there was nothing inside but a small handcrafted metal box with a lock on it. I grabbed it and ran for my car. Before I reached it, half a dozen men came out of hiding and opened fire." His head whipped toward her.

She'd almost died that day. "I ducked behind my car. Forced them back. But not before one man almost took me out." He'd been inches from her when she'd shot him. "I jumped into the car and got away." Victoria had ditched the car. Found another. Traveled over a thousand miles before fatigue forced her to seek refuge in an abandoned farmhouse outside of a small Texas town. She'd thought she'd be safe. Only nothing had been further from the truth. She'd fallen asleep out of sheer exhaustion and been awakened to the sound of a chopper hovering overhead.

With the box in one hand and David's Glock in the other, she rushed out to her car, reached for the door and spotted something terrifying. A bomb had been planted there, set up to explode when she opened the door.

If it hadn't been for God's guidance, she wouldn't have escaped. The first chance she'd gotten, Victoria had made sure there was no tracking device among her possessions. Then she'd ended up near the West Kootenai Amish community in Montana. Renting the cabin seemed like a wise move. No one from the CIA knew anything about her Amish past or her former last name, except for David. Her mother's *Englisch* cousin had adopted her and changed her surname to Parrish. She'd been so certain going off the grid in such a remote setting would keep her safe. She'd been wrong.

Victoria scrubbed an unsteady hand across her forehead. Even if she could get the evidence out of the cabin, it might not matter. If she couldn't escape the men coming after her, she'd be dead before the truth about David's death was ever known.

Victoria stopped suddenly, and her arm barred the path in front of Aaron. Before he could ask what was wrong, she held a finger against her lips and pointed in front of them. He caught a glimpse of a cabin through the thick foliage. One more step remained, and it would be the most difficult.

Keeping his heart rate at a steady pace was next to impossible as he thought about what might be waiting for them there. As much as he wanted to think it was as easy as grabbing the box and leaving, the tension between his shoulders wouldn't let him cling to that hope.

Something snagged his attention right away. Voices. Not coming from the cabin, but closer. The men guarding the cabin had heard the commotion from earlier and were coming to investigate.

Victoria grabbed his arm and tugged him, along with her, out of sight. Several people were approaching.

Aaron spotted his and Victoria's footprints in the snow. "We cannot stay here," he whispered against her ear and pointed to them. "It won't take the men long to see those."

She started walking again at a fast pace. This area was a protected national forest. The trees here were not harvested regularly and grew thick and tall in search of sunlight. They'd have to battle the undergrowth to get through, but so would the people coming after them.

"Listen." Victoria cocked her head to one side. It appeared the men had reached the spot where he and Victoria had entered the woods.

"They've seen our footprints. It won't take them long to find our trail."

These men would know she had come back to the cabin for something important.

"Do you trust me?" Victoria asked, holding his gaze.

He didn't have to think about his answer. "Of course. I trust you with my life."

She slowly smiled and squeezed his hands as if his answer meant the world to her. "Thank you. I know a way we can reach the cabin by going in from a different direction." She headed right and he followed.

The cold burned Aaron's chest. All he could think about was his *sohn*. He prayed for *Gott's* protection for his family.

"I see it." They were close to the mountains bordering her cabin. At one time, Aaron knew every square inch of the land by heart. He and his brothers had hunted there all their lives. The cabin she'd rented had once belonged to a relative. He and his family had come here often when Aaron was a boy.

Victoria stopped so suddenly that Aaron almost slammed into her.

"What is wrong?"

She pointed to the cabin. Half a dozen men stood guard. With others combing the woods behind them, they couldn't risk trying to get the evidence now. Like it or not, they had to save themselves. Retrieving the box would have to wait for another day.

"If we don't leave now, we'll be cut off," he told her. "Those men behind us will catch up with us soon."

She glanced toward the cabin and he could almost read her mind. The proof she so desperately needed was close, and yet they were being forced to leave it behind.

After a moment of hesitation, she nodded. "You're right. How do we get back to the buggy?"

It had been a while since Aaron had come this way. It took a second to gather his bearings. If they followed the river that cut through the wilderness, the sound would muffle their movements and hopefully allow them to reach the buggy undetected. Unless the men had found it already and had stationed people there to ambush them. The thought was chilling.

Aaron shoved aside branches and trudged through the thick brush littered with downed trees, while doubts rose in his head. Was this the right direction? It had been years since he'd been this way and things had grown quite a bit.

After walking for some time, the noise of the rushing water was a welcome sound. The river came into view while an uneasy feeling settled in Aaron's stomach.

Somewhere nearby, a tree branch snapped. Aaron swung back to Victoria. She'd stopped walking and was staring at something with a look of horror on her face.

"Run!" she yelled. Before Aaron had time to react, a man appeared out of nowhere. He held something in his hand. A rifle.

"Aaron, watch out!" Victoria screamed. But the warning came too late. The man pulled the trigger. Aaron's eyes closed briefly expecting the pain of a gunshot. Nothing happened. The gun had jammed.

Denki, Gott!

Aaron ran toward the man. He had to take the weapon away before this man shot at him again. Aaron grabbed for the weapon, but the man shoved Aaron hard and tried to get the gun in position to fire again. Aaron wrestled for control of the weapon once more. The gun went off with a deafening blast. Pain ripped through Aaron's shoulder. He fell backwards, his head slamming against a rock. The world around him disappeared, as if someone had slammed a door firmly on his consciousness.

FIVE

"Aaron!" Victoria watched in horror as he fell to the ground and stopped moving. The shot had hit its mark. How bad were his injuries? No matter what, she had to help him.

She fired off several rounds, sending the shooter into hiding. The second he was out of sight, she charged for where Aaron was lying. After grabbing him underneath the arms, she heaved him off the ground and stumbled over every step as she dragged him away.

This was all her fault. She'd been so determined that nothing would stand in the way of her getting the proof. Because of her stubbornness, she'd gotten Aaron hurt.

With her heart pumping hard, she struggled to keep from falling. She'd only bought herself a temporary reprieve. Slowing down wasn't an option.

The noise of the water grew louder, drowning out her frantic pulse. A gunshot ricocheted through the air and lodged in a tree near her head. Victoria hit the ground and crawled to the closest tree, pulling Aaron along with her with one arm. With the other, she returned fire.

Several more men joined the shooter. She was now overwhelmingly outnumbered.

If she stayed here, she didn't stand a chance. Both she and Aaron would be dead. The only way to save his life was to draw away their attention. She managed to get Aaron's heavy body behind some scrub brush and out of sight, but the effort quickly depleted her remaining strength. She gathered a lungful of air and stumbled into a run, her injured leg making each step difficult. Victoria kept as low as possible. It was her they wanted. She was counting on them following her and leaving Aaron behind for now.

The noise of the river drowned out all other sound. The men could be right on top of her and she wouldn't know it. A glance behind proved they were still coming.

Frantic, she ran harder, her arms pumping at her sides, the rifle in her hand. Her dress bunched around her legs. The strings of her prayer *kapp* billowed out behind her.

She searched the water's edge for some way out and found none. The river was close to overflowing its banks. It cut a wide swath through the wilderness in front of her.

They were closing in quickly and she was trapped. Hopelessness threatened to snuff her out.

As she watched the raging water, the solution became clear. Did she have it in her to survive this?

While her faith faltered, the enemy closed in. The woods exploded with gunfire. She hit the ground hard. Pain surged up her wounded leg. Victoria scrambled to the nearest tree and fired over her shoulder. One man screamed, but there were plenty more pursuers.

She emptied the rifle and tossed it aside, then dragged out the handgun she'd taken. The magazine held seven bullets. She still had David's trusted Glock, which would allow her to stand her ground for a while.

Victoria peeked out from behind the tree. Two men eased closer. She shot several times, forcing them back. This was a battle she wouldn't win. Before long, she'd be surrounded. She had a decision to make. Only it wasn't really a decision at all. If she stood a chance at surviving, she would have to go into the water and do her best to live.

The men continued to advance through the trees. They were almost on top of her. She emptied the handgun she'd taken off her previous attacker into the space between them and tossed it aside before grabbing David's Glock. An eerie silence followed. Where were they? Close? Slowly, she eased toward the water's edge, praying she would survive. A hail of shots flew past her. "I'm sorry, Aaron. So sorry."

A noise he couldn't define sent Aaron's eyes flying open. He sat up quickly, wincing at his throbbing head. His left shoulder felt as if hot coals were being pressed against it. He grabbed it and pain shot down from the contact.

He closed his eyes as the drilling in his head intensified and struggled to keep from being sick. When the nausea faded and his vision cleared, he drew back his hand, which was covered in blood. Then he remembered. He'd been shot. Where was Victoria?

Aaron stumbled to his feet as the noises continued. He realized they were gunshots coming from close to the river. He was no longer where he'd been when the attack occurred. Someone had moved him. Victoria. She was in danger. He pulled out the handgun he'd tucked inside his jacket.

With his head pounding out each step, Aaron ran toward the shooting while he fought against the foggy feeling that turned his stomach. No matter what, he couldn't let them hurt her.

As he drew closer, barrel flashes lit up the

twilight of the woods. He was almost right on top of the men. The woods were crawling with them. The river came into view. Where was Victoria?

"Give yourself up, Parrish!" an unrecognizable voice called out.

Parrish? Aaron squinted through the gun's smoke until he saw her standing near the water's edge. The man was speaking to her, but she'd told him her last name was Kauffman.

His mind tried to make sense of what was happening. Victoria moved toward the water. He screamed for her to stop, but his voice was drowned out by the sound of bullets.

As he looked on in horror, Victoria jumped into the frigid river and went under quickly. The rushing waters swept her out of sight. He had to do something to save her. Aaron skirted past the area where the men had gone to the water's edge and were searching to make sure she was dead. The thought was sickening.

"She can't survive in those waters. Let's take care of him and get out of here."

Aaron froze, then moved to hide behind a tree. They couldn't afford to leave any witnesses behind.

Several men passed close to him. Every second Victoria was in the water, her chances of survival slipped away. All Aaron wanted to do was go after her, but if he was discovered, he'd be dead.

When the last person disappeared, Aaron slipped from behind the tree and ran. If he could reach the place where the river bent, there was a chance he could pull her from the water in time. The river ran high from the fall floods. If he missed her at the bend, she'd be gone.

With his chest burning, he waded through thick brush close to the water's edge and scanned its silvery surface. Where was she? Was he too late?

Frantic, he charged farther down the riverbank to where a tree had fallen into the water. Brush and branches were lodged there, too. And something else. He caught sight of the blue of her dress and fought his way through thick mud to reach her. Her prayer *kapp* had come free and was caught in some briars.

She wasn't moving and her weak pulse terrified him. Aaron shoved the weapon in his coat pocket and quickly removed it. He placed it around her for warmth before he lifted her into his arms. Pain flared down from the place where the bullet had torn through his shoulder, and he almost dropped her.

Aaron shifted her weight away from the injured arm and realized she held something in her hand. Her weapon. She'd managed to hold onto it despite the rushing water.

He untangled the gun from her fingers and tucked it into the waist of his pants, then scrambled up the bank while praying the noise wouldn't bring unwelcome attention to their location. All he could think about was reaching the buggy. The blankets there would provide added warmth. Would it be enough to save her?

As he topped the riverbank, Victoria slowly opened her eyes.

Relief flooded his body as he sought to reassure her. "You are *oke*. You're safe, but you must stay as quiet as possible. Right now, they think you are dead, and they are searching for me to kill me. We don't have much time."

Her eyes widened against her pale face. Aaron snugged his coat closer around her. He was worried about the effects of the cold water on her body.

"I can walk," she said in a raspy whisper and tried to free herself, but he shook his head.

"Just rest."

Without answering, she closed her eyes and laid her head against his shoulder. His protective instincts rose inside him and his arms tightened around her. Though he only knew a little about her life, he felt more connected to her than he did most people, including his family. The guilt she carried matched his own. They were alike in many ways.

As he neared the buggy, the mare's nickering caught his attention. Almost there. Aaron pushed through the overgrowth with a renewed burst of energy. The sight of the buggy through the trees was a welcome one. He huffed out a huge sigh of relief.

Victoria's troubled gaze latched onto his face as if she was expecting danger.

"We've reached the buggy," he told her. The mare spotted them and whinnied. Never was there a more joyful sound, but they were far from being out of danger. By now, the men would have realized he'd escaped. They'd keep looking for him because letting him live wasn't an option. He'd seen too much.

Aaron gently placed Victoria on the seat and grabbed the two blankets. He wrapped them snug around her slender body and prayed they would provide enough warmth to keep her safe until he reached Hunter's home.

With haste, he climbed on board and guided the nervous mare from her hiding place. Aaron clamped onto the reins and did his best to control the anxious animal. He didn't dare make a verbal command for fear it would alert the men to their location. As it was, the noise the mare was making couldn't be disguised.

The horse finally settled down enough for Aaron to ease her toward a little-traveled path used mostly by the people of the Amish community. Once they'd covered some distance without being found, Aaron allowed himself to relax.

"Where will this direction take us?"

"Eventually back to Hunter's place, but it will take longer this way. I don't think it's safe to travel the main roads."

She nodded but the tension on her face didn't go away. "Where is my Glock? I had it with me when I went into the water."

Aaron handed her the weapon and watched as she pointed the barrel down.

"What are you doing?" he asked curiously.

"I'm letting the water run out of the firing-pin channel and the barrel." She popped out the magazine and let the water drain from it. "These guns are virtually indestructible, but if the ammo gets wet, it's useless."

She leaned forward slightly, her attention intent on the upcoming countryside. He could almost read her thoughts. She'd be planning another trip back to the cabin as soon as possible. Not that he could blame her. After what happened back there, he was positive whatever was in the box her partner left was huge. And these men knew it.

He placed his hand on her arm. "We will figure it out."

She shifted toward him and noticed the way he favored his shoulder. "Aaron, you're hurt. With everything that happened, I'd forgotten you were shot. How bad is it?"

He had no way of knowing the extent of the injury, but the bullet had embedded itself near where the first bullet had grazed.

Aaron looked at her worried expression and tried not to worry her. "It's not serious. We can look at it once we reach Hunter's place."

She scrubbed her palms across her eyes. "I'm so sorry, Aaron. I cannot believe the extremes these men are willing to go to just to ensure their secrets stay hidden."

He tamped down his growing anger. That there were people in the world capable of such violence was unbelievable. "Whatever they're hiding, they must be exposed. We can't let them win. We have to stop them."

She held his gaze. The concern on her face was all for him and he stopped her before she could speak the words aloud. "I know what you're going to say, but this *is* my fight, Victoria. These men are trying to kill you and they've put my family in the middle of their evil plans. I am part of this. Let me help you find the truth."

SIX

Victoria pulled in an unsteady breath. She couldn't look away from this handsome and sincere man. He'd been through so much himself with losing his wife, and yet he stood strong and protective of his family…and of her, though she didn't deserve his protection. Aaron personified all the things her mother had told her about her father. Things she'd once dreamed of having in her life.

His gaze slowly traveled over her face and her chest tightened as she struggled to reclaim control of whatever was happening between them. She had a mission to finish. Nothing could stand in her way. Not even Aaron.

She turned away and tried to calm her frantic pulse. They were worlds apart. This wasn't her life anymore. Once this was finished, she'd leave West Kootenai and find her place somewhere in the sun. Life for Aaron would return to normal.

A quick glance behind them proved the same thing it had two minutes earlier: no one had followed them. She tried to believe she was just checking to make sure they weren't being followed, yet the truth was, she needed the small action as a distraction while she pulled herself together. Being back among the Amish—being with Aaron—was wreaking havoc on her emotions. She had to get a grip.

No matter how much she might wish differently, she couldn't bring back the innocent girl she'd once been. Couldn't erase the dreadful things she'd done for justice—things this simple existence and this gentle man beside her would never condone.

When she turned back, she found Aaron still watching her, no doubt curious about her sudden silence. He was probably wondering what she was thinking. Best not to open that door.

"We should be safe enough on this path." He'd misunderstood her silence for worry and she let him.

The mare kept a steady pace down the narrow way. Victoria tried to shut out the things she'd once wanted. It was hard when everywhere she looked was a reminder, including the man seated next to her.

Though he'd risk his safety for her, she knew so little about Aaron's life, other than that they'd both lost someone close to them. She wanted to hear his story. Hers had been gnawing at her heart, dragging her down with survivor's guilt. Why David? The others? Why not her?

She shoved everything down into the dark hole where it rested on good days.

"Your mother told me about your wife passing." Victoria watched his eyebrows raise at her comment. He was probably confused as to why she chose to bring up his wife out of the blue. Maybe she needed a reminder that they both were still in mourning.

"She told me these were her clothes. I'm sorry, Aaron. I know how hard it is to lose someone you love. People tell you that you can't stop living your life, but it's hard, isn't it?"

His jaw flexed several times. "*Jah*, it is. Irene has been gone for almost a year, and yet there are days I still can't believe she's dead." His voice was thick with pain as if it had just happened.

She remembered the day David drew his last breath. He'd been in a coma for weeks when he'd suddenly awakened. She'd recovered from her injuries enough to be at his side. He looked her straight in the eyes and whispered those disturbing words before he passed.

In the days following, she'd been on autopilot. David and the rest of her fallen teammates had been sent stateside for burial. She'd collected his belongings and was supposed to turn them in to Command, but with everything that had happened, she'd forgotten.

There was no doubt in her mind her oversight had been a direction from God. After the first incident, when she'd been run off the road outside of Langley, she hadn't thought much of it until someone shot at her. The bullet had come close enough to graze her cheek. She'd known then that whatever David had discovered was enough to get him killed. And her.

Victoria dragged in a deep breath and pushed aside those memories.

"How did your wife pass?" she asked, desperate to get out of her own head. Too much ugliness and blame lived there.

Aaron kept his focus straight ahead. For the longest time she wondered if he'd heard her.

"She had cancer and I had no idea how truly ill she was until it was too late." Each word carried a wealth of guilt.

He turned and she found herself drowning in the tidal wave of heartache in his eyes.

"Some cancers are hard to detect," she said gently. "You can't blame yourself—"

A bitter laugh cut her answer short. "*Nay*, I should have known. She was my *fraa*, but I was too busy trying to keep the business going after my *daed's* passing. Our family was falling apart. I thought I could fix it all." He gripped the reins tighter. "But I couldn't. No matter how hard I tried, or how long I worked, I couldn't."

She tentatively touched his arm. "Sometimes, no matter what you do, you can't save the ones you love."

His shoulders slumped. As he pushed out a ragged breath, his desperate eyes found hers. "The one person I should have saved I did not. Irene didn't want to be a burden. She knew how hard I was working, so she kept the illness from me until it was too late. By the time I noticed the weight loss—the sickness—she had days to live."

"Oh, Aaron, I'm so sorry." Losing David had been like a knife to her heart, but with their type of work, death was always a possibility.

"Her dying wish was that I do not grieve too long," he said so softly she almost didn't hear. "She worried about everyone except herself."

"I'm sure she would be proud of how you've cared for your son and your mother." Yet the words felt inadequate. She'd been so focused on her troubles that she hadn't realized the suffering this strong man beside her had gone through.

Up ahead, what appeared to be a gravel road intersected the path they were traveling. Aaron stopped the buggy long enough to make sure no one was coming before he guided the mare out and to the left.

An uncomfortable silence stretched out between them. Victoria struggled for something to say to end it. Aaron's story had struck a chord with her. She, of all people, understood the feeling of guilt attached to losing someone close.

On the horizon, a car approached from the opposite direction, its lights blinding in the twilight. Shielding her eyes, Victoria sat up straighter. Aaron had told her this road was less traveled than most. The likelihood of meeting another buggy was slim, much less a car.

She grabbed his arm. "We're in trouble." There was no doubt in her mind—the vehicle heading straight for them was part of the team sent to take her out.

"They've seen us. It's too late to get off the road." He covered her hand. "We don't know if the driver is part of it. Try to relax. We don't wish to alert them any more than necessary."

Aaron struggled with his own misgivings. He should have waited longer before entering the road. Should have listened for any noise. Instead he'd been too caught up with the tragedies of his past to think clearly, and because of it, he'd put them in a possibly deadly situation.

Victoria slipped the blanket from around her shoulders and covered her silver-blond hair from view.

"Keep your head down," she told him.

Aaron tugged his hat lower and kept his eyes on the road as the car eased past them. Three men were seated inside. They all watched him and Victoria with suspicion. The vehicle cleared the back of the buggy and continued down the road. "I don't think they recognized us."

The car disappeared past the rise. Aaron gripped the reins tight to keep her from seeing the tremors in his hands. "Did any of them look familiar?" If these were her people, then surely some of them would be familiar.

She shook her head. "And I'm positive they weren't any of the men who attacked us near the cabin. Or from what I could tell, they weren't at the river, either."

The men near the riverbank would still believe her dead. But if these men who had just passed them were part of the team sent to kill Victoria, they'd know what she looked like. A blanket covering her hair wouldn't keep them from knowing it was her. "We need to get off this road as quick as possible."

Aaron urged the mare into a faster pace. "There's an abandoned farm a little ways from here. We can hide out there."

Once they topped the next hill, Aaron looked behind them. The car had stopped on the side of the road. "Oh, no."

Victoria's head snapped to look behind them. "They're turning around." She held his gaze. "Hurry, Aaron."

The buggy lurched down the hill and out of sight for the moment. The old Glick place was not too far. Would they make it in time?

He spotted the drive and turned the mare onto it. Darkness descended quickly in the winter months. It would work in their favor and help to conceal the buggy tracks.

Aaron drove past the decaying house to the barn. "Whoa, mare," he said in a firm voice. The horse whinnied her protest but obeyed. "We have a better chance of staying hidden if the buggy is out of sight. I'll get the door. Can you pull it inside?"

Victoria took the reins from him. Aaron hopped down and hurried to the door. A board served as a latch to hold it closed. It had been years since anyone lived here. The wood was warped from many a cold winter. He struggled to free it.

When it finally gave way, the door dragged across the ground as he opened it, leaving a mark in the snow. Would they notice?

Victoria eased the mare into the cavernous

space, and Aaron quickly shut the door behind them. It was pitch-black. He felt his way to the buggy.

"Take my hand." The only sound in the place was the mare's labored breathing. In the darkness, Victoria slipped her hand in his and he guided her down next to him.

"They could have followed us." Her gentle breath fanned across his face, her closeness a major distraction. He could feel her watching him through the darkness. Did she feel this way, too?

After another second passed without a word, Victoria headed out the smaller side door. He touched the handgun in his coat pocket. The cold steel barrel gave him a measure of peace. The silence of the settling night was broken by the noise of a car's engine approaching.

"That's close," Victoria whispered. "If they see the tracks… We should keep moving."

She was right, but they couldn't afford to take the buggy through the densely treed countryside surrounding the Glick property.

The car's headlights became visible through the trees. Aaron's thoughts swirled. "If we unharness the mare, we'll make better time riding her out than walking."

She didn't hesitate. "Let's do it."

Aaron turned on his heel and headed back

to the barn. "We'll go through the woods and cut across the neighbor's property to keep from being followed. It will take us longer to reach Hunter's place, but we'll be traveling in the dark, and they will be forced to use the roads around the community. They shouldn't be able to follow us. Help me get the mare free."

The darkness inside the structure made it a struggle to free the mare. Once she was loose, Aaron led her out through the side door and to the rotting front porch.

Headlights swept onto the drive. The car would be there in a matter of minutes.

Aaron kept a close eye on the advancing vehicle while holding the mare still. Victoria stood on the top step and swung her leg across the horse's back. He handed her the reins and did the same.

Riding bareback was challenging in the daylight—at night it would be dangerous. But they didn't have a choice.

He took the reins back. The bright lights of the vehicle hit them both. The driver spotted them and sped up.

"Lean forward. I have you," Aaron told her and nudged the mare's sides. Victoria edged forward and tangled her hand in its mane. Aaron placed one arm around her waist and leaned against her.

"Go, mare." The animal responded quickly and headed for the woods. As they reached the first group of trees, they both sat up.

The car screeched to a stop near where they'd entered. Doors slammed shut. A terrifying silence followed and then the entire countryside lit up with weapons firing.

"They're coming after us," Victoria shouted above the noise. The mare bolted into a frenzied gallop, away from the danger. Aaron grabbed the reins tight and held on to Victoria as they raced through the dark night into what he hoped would be their freedom.

Muzzle flashes ignited behind them once more. The men weren't giving up.

"Stay low," Aaron yelled over the noise. Victoria leaned against the animal's mane once more. The spooked mare charged through the woods as bullets whizzed past them. Aaron did his best to keep them astride while trying to keep the mare from slamming into a tree. One stray bullet and the horse would be incapacitated. They'd be on their own with an unknown number of men coming after them with one goal in mind—ending both their lives.

SEVEN

It sounded as if they were in the middle of a war. Bullets continued to pepper the trees. The mare snorted wildly and galloped at a frightening pace through the darkness, guided only by her instincts. And Victoria prayed like she never had before.

Soon, the gunfire became fainter. The animal put distance between them and the shooters.

Aaron sat up and Victoria did the same. He pulled back on the reins to get the mare to realize the danger had passed enough to slow.

"That was close." Victoria looked behind them. Nothing but darkness. Still, she didn't believe for a second the men would give up.

"We've outrun them for now. But they are determined, and they want us dead." Aaron's words sent a chill down her spine. She had no idea what she'd involved them in.

"So far, nothing about what's happening makes sense. The evidence David left is just a bunch of surveillance photos of something being moved through the desert in a truck. There are a couple taken showing a meeting with half a dozen men at night. And one of what appears to be a ledger of some sort, but all that's there is—a bunch of numbers that I don't understand." She shook her head. What was their significance?

"These surveillance photos were taken in another country?"

His arm circling her waist was a comfort. The clean outdoor scent of him reminded her of her childhood here in Montana. She still recalled the smell of the pine trees. The snow at Christmas. Her mother's smile. Sometimes, when she closed her eyes, she could almost picture her mother's pretty face.

With tomorrow being Christmas Eve, the peace this season represented was so far out of her reach that she couldn't imagine a time when she wouldn't be on the run.

Exhaustion made it hard to collect her thoughts. "They were taken in Afghanistan, but I have no idea when, or how David got them into the storage unit." She shook her head. "David and I, along with our team, were there to try to turn someone. Our commander, Trevor Hawk, believed the asset would be able to supply information about the massive amounts of heroin being smuggled from the country." They'd gone out into the desert that night to meet with him because he was afraid of being identified and killed. When they'd reached the location, three of their five-man team had gone inside. She'd heard a sound nearby in a burned-out structure that alarmed her and had gone to check it out. David went, too. When they'd found nothing, they went after their teammates. Then the world around them exploded. She and David were badly injured. The rest of the team were killed.

"You think there were drugs in those vehicles?"

"It's possible," she said with a sigh. "The only question is what is so important about these drugs being moved. It happens frequently in that country. There's big money in heroin." She had no idea what David was trying to tell her or how it connected to the bombing.

A field appeared in front of them. "Where are we?" she asked, because she'd lost her bearings.

"This land belongs to Hunter's neighbor. It's not far to my brother's house now. We should be safe there."

If only she could believe that, but until the truth was known, she'd never be safe from the men coming after her.

Aaron's arm tightened around her waist. "I

believe we're getting closer to the truth." His deep voice reassured her. He'd weathered many storms in his life and yet he was still standing. Perhaps there was hope for her.

"I really miss this way of life." Her inner thoughts slipped out and she realized she'd spoken them aloud.

"This way of life?" he asked in surprise. "But how would you know about our ways?"

She smiled. "I know because I was once Amish." She hadn't told another soul about being Amish since David. "It's one of the reasons why I came here to hide. I lived in the St. Ignatius community until I was five and my mother passed away." Saying the words out loud brought back the hurt. "I went to live with *Englischers* after her death. Kauffman was my Amish surname. When I was adopted, my new family changed my last name to Parrish. I began using Kauffman again after I escaped the storage facility because no one else knows about my Amish past. I thought it would help keep me safe." She shook her head. "I was wrong."

Seconds passed. She couldn't imagine what was going through his head. "I had no idea you were once Amish. Now I understand how you know so much about our faith."

"I'd almost forgotten how special this way of life truly is."

Aaron eased the mare from the tree coverage and into the field. A house appeared in front of them, with a lantern's glow visible through the windows. A woodstove puffed white smoke into the night air. The picture-perfect sight filled her with longing. This was the life she'd lost, the one she'd thought was not possible again.

For the longest time after she'd left St. Ignatius, Victoria felt as if she didn't belong anywhere. She drifted through school and college. When she was recruited for the CIA, she believed she'd found her place at last. Somewhere that she could make a difference and help others who felt lost like she had. But each new mission chipped away a little more of her soul. It took losing David to make her realize, this wasn't the life she longed for. She wanted one she'd lost. Was it possible? Could she go back to the person she was all those years ago? Would she be able to live the simple life she'd once shared with her mother and put the horrible things she'd done in the name of justice behind her? Or had the cold-blooded killer that existed inside her taken away her chance for redemption?

Holding back his surprise was impossible. She'd once been Amish, until that life had been taken from her, along with the mother she loved. Losing her family had turned Victoria into the person she was today. Was that little girl from long ago still in there somewhere?

Being close to her—seeing glimpses of the caring woman that still existed despite the things she'd been through—teased him with possibilities he'd thought were gone from his life.

Victoria was a beautiful woman, but she was just as scarred as he was. And her life was nothing like his. Best to let go of that hope because it would only lead to pain.

He'd told her they were safe, and yet he didn't feel anything close to it. All he could think about was their narrow escape. These men weren't going to give up without being stopped.

"Let's stay clear of the Grabers' house. I don't want to alarm them, and we should keep them out of this." He guided the mare away from the small farmhouse where the older couple lived. The last thing he wanted was to bring this danger to such innocent people.

He nodded to the right. "Hunter's place is beyond those woods."

"I hope they haven't somehow connected Hunter with you. By now, they'll know your name and will be looking for anyone connected to you."

What she said settled uneasily around him. It was impossible for him to grasp, but he had no idea how these men worked. "You are certain they are with the CIA?" It seemed unimaginable that these men would betray the country they vowed to protect.

She nodded, her hair brushing his face. "Without a doubt. They are highly trained, and they have unimaginable technology that allows them to be able to locate us anywhere. I don't know how long it will be safe for us to stay at Hunter's."

The thought of the men searching his family's homes was unsettling.

The mare continued through the woods where the temperature hovered below freezing. Before, he'd thought it too dangerous to go after the evidence with so many armed men roaming around. Now, he believed there was no other choice.

After they cleared the trees, the side of Hunter's house came into view. Aaron couldn't imagine how worried his family would be.

He took the horse to the barn and hopped down. Aaron put his hands around Victoria's waist and eased her to the ground.

Inches separated them, and she was close enough for him to see all her doubts, feel her uncertainty. She swallowed deeply and bit her bottom lip, pulling his attention to her mouth. Her blond hair had escaped its bun and hung loose. He tucked a strand behind her ear and watched her draw in a breath and search his face, looking for answers he couldn't give.

Victoria had survived freezing waters, armed men bent on taking her life and a frantic ride on the back of a mare without a saddle. She was as tough as anyone he'd met before and yet there was something vulnerable about her that made him want to protect her. He hadn't been drawn to another woman in this way in a long time, and it felt as if he was betraying Irene.

The very thought cut deep and he stepped back abruptly. "Let me get the mare inside the barn and then let's warm up. You've been through enough today." He didn't look at her as he opened the barn door. After leading the horse to one of the stalls, he fed her some oats while he tried to shut the woman waiting for him near the door out of his head. She was an *Englischer* and not part of his world any longer. Once this terrible thing ended, she would return to her world. And he had his *sohn* to consider.

After he filled the horse's water trough, he joined Victoria by the door. She stepped away when he drew close. He'd hurt her and that had never been his intention.

Victoria stopped suddenly and pointed.

He saw what she did. A car was parked off to the far side of the house, away from the barn.

An *Englischer* was in the house with his whole family.

Raised voices came from inside. Victoria tugged him to the woods behind the barn and out of sight.

"I don't recognize the car, do you?"

Aaron continued to watch the house. "No, it isn't the same as the one from the road. My family is in danger. We both know what these men are capable of doing."

He headed for the clearing, but she grabbed his arm. "You can't go in there, Aaron. They're looking for you and me. So far, they don't know your brothers and they've only seen your mother and son briefly. They might not connect them to us. Chances are, they're searching at random and hoping someone from the community is hiding us. If you charge in there now, you could get someone hurt."

He swung toward her. "That's my family in there. These men are dangerous."

"I know that, but the best way to help them now is to stay out of sight."

Standing by and doing nothing was unthinkable, but if he charged in and confronted the men, he'd be putting everyone's lives in danger.

The heated conversation carried from inside the house. Hunter was speaking with someone...and the other voice sounded familiar.

The front door flew open and slammed against the wall. "If you're lying, we'll be back, and when we are, it won't be good for you or your family. We'll have you arrested for harboring a fugitive. You all will be jailed." Aaron finally recognized the voice. Logan.

Four men stormed from the house, and his brothers stepped out onto the porch behind them.

One man took several menacing steps toward Aaron's brothers with his fist raised like a weapon before he turned to the goons standing by. "You two, stay here with them. If they aren't telling the truth…shoot them."

EIGHT

Victoria couldn't imagine Aaron's reaction to hearing these men threaten his family.

"They're going to kill them!" The horror on his face was hard to take, but they couldn't engage in a shoot-out with so many innocent people around.

She grabbed his arm and held him back when he would have charged from their hiding place.

"If you go after them you could put your family in the middle of a gunfight."

Two men had reached the barn already. Flashlight beams moved along the ground. How long before their footprints were spotted?

"We have to get out of sight." She pulled him deeper into the woods while the men continued searching.

"Someone's been here recently. I have two sets of footprints," one of the men by the barn said, alerting the others.

Victoria didn't slow down. Seeing anything

in front of them in the darkness was impossible. One false move and they'd go down.

Several people entered the woods, tramping through the underbrush. She and Aaron would never be able to outrun the men and they'd be heard if they tried.

"They're almost right on top of us. Hide," she whispered and frantically searched for someplace to get out of sight. "Over there." She and Aaron ducked beneath some brush.

Victoria checked the Glock. It was completely dry, and the magazine held half a clip. Bullets were precious. She didn't have enough to take on the enemy. Their only chance at living was to stay hidden.

Multiple footsteps halted close to them. Victoria held her breath. Would they be discovered?

"There's too much underbrush to pick up their trail." This from the same man she'd heard barking orders earlier. Logan.

"This is the Amish man's family. There's a good chance he'll return for them. Are you going to tell him we quit, because I sure don't want to be the one?" The second man's voice wasn't familiar. "You know what he's capable of doing." A chill made its way up Victoria's spine. Who was this man they spoke of with such fear?

"We're not quitting. Let's keep going. If they're in the woods, we'll find them," Logan said.

The men's footsteps faded as they continued through the woods, flashlights panning all around.

Victoria knelt beside Aaron. They couldn't afford to make a single sound, or the men would hear them.

She did her best to control her labored breathing as they waited. After many tense minutes, the two men could be heard tromping through the woods toward them once more. Victoria grabbed Aaron's hand and clutched it tight when they stopped close to their hiding spot.

"Let's go back to the others and check out the next property. They're hiding somewhere in the community. We're going to find them if we have to search every house around," Logan ordered.

Feet shuffled inches from where they crouched.

"I don't know. What if they are watching the place, waiting for us to leave?"

Victoria's gaze shot to Aaron.

"If they come back here, we'll get them. I'm stationing two of our people at the end of the drive toward the road and out of sight. They can keep an eye on the place from a distance in case she and the Amish man return."

After what seemed like forever, the men headed back toward the house. Soon, the car's engine fired, and the vehicle left.

Victoria slowly rose from her cramped position and held out her hand to Aaron. They moved through the woods while worst-case scenarios played through her mind. What if it had all been a ruse to lure them out of hiding?

She kept in the trees until they were close to the back of the house so that the men watching from the road wouldn't see.

"Wait here. I'll check around back to make sure there's no one there." Aaron started through the trees to the clearing near the rear of the house.

"I'm coming with you." She didn't wait for him to protest.

Once they reached the house, Aaron stepped up on the porch and glanced through the window. "I don't see anyone." He knocked quietly once.

While he waited by the door, Victoria slipped around the side. No one was there, either. Still, with the men guarding the road, leaving that way would no longer be an option.

She went back to where Aaron stood. A single set of footsteps moved toward the door. She gripped the Glock tight. Someone peeked past the curtains on the window near the door.

A couple of heartbeats passed, then the door opened. Fletcher stepped out onto the back porch.

"Thank You, *Gott,*" he whispered with heartfelt relief. "I thought those men had returned."

The extent of what he and his family had gone through was clear on his worried face.

Fletcher looked nervously around before ushering them inside. "*Komm.* Quickly. I fear they are still watching the house." He fumbled with the lock until it caught.

"They are." Aaron told him about what he and Victoria had overheard. "They have people near the road."

Fletcher watched them with fear on his face. His gaze latched onto the dried blood on his brother's shoulder. "You've been shot." The shock in his voice was clear.

"It's not serious," Aaron assured him.

Fletcher hurried to the living room and closed the curtains. Once all the interior rooms were no longer visible from outside, Aaron and Victoria followed Fletcher.

"What did those men want?" Aaron asked his brother.

Fletcher looked to Victoria. "They wanted you. They seemed convinced you were here somewhere. They knew Hunter and I were Aaron's brothers." The men had done their homework.

"Daed!" young Caleb exclaimed and bolted from his seat to throw himself at his father.

Aaron winced as the boy grabbed hold of him. She could tell his shoulder was giving him grief despite his claims otherwise. She'd caused this. Aaron had almost died because of her.

Tears filled the boy's eyes. "They said you'd done something bad. They said you were in a lot of trouble."

"They are not telling the truth. Those men were lying." Aaron gathered his son close. "But we must be as quiet as possible, Caleb. There are men watching the house from down the drive. We don't want them to know that Victoria and I are here."

Over the top of Caleb's head, Aaron held her gaze. "And neither Victoria nor I have done anything wrong." He wanted her to believe what took place wasn't her fault, but if she hadn't brought her troubles to Aaron, none of this would have happened. The longer she remained here, the more likely it was someone would get hurt. And it was only a matter of time before those men struck out on locating them and returned to Hunter's home for answers.

"You're freezing." Martha came up beside Victoria and wrapped a quilt around her shoulders. "*Komm* warm yourself by the fire." Martha urged her into one of the chairs in front of the fire. "I will get you both something to eat. You must be starved."

Victoria smiled at Martha's kindness and snugged the quilt closer around her body. Together with the warmth of the fire, it made the chill slowly subside.

You know what he's capable of doing...

She couldn't let go of what the one man had said. Who was this person they spoke about? Was he the one responsible for ordering David's death?

A shiver passed between her shoulder blades as she considered the possibility that these men, led by an unknown person, were using the CIA resources to smuggle heroin from Afghanistan. Somehow, they'd discovered David was on to them and believed she possessed some information that would bring them down. They couldn't afford to stop until the threat she posed was eliminated.

Victoria glanced at the simple signs of the coming holiday scattered around the room. They were pretty much the same as what she'd seen at Aaron's home—a few handmade cards and some candles. Christmas for the Amish was celebrated with few decorations, but filled with family and friends.

She imagined the Christmas meal Aaron's family would enjoy and the church service that would no doubt be held on December 25. The day after would be one of relaxing and visiting others.

A pang of jealousy reminded her that but

for circumstances, this might be her life. She couldn't imagine what it must be like to have a big family like Aaron's.

Victoria blew out a weary breath that seemed to come straight from her soul. No matter what happened, if she survived this, she could never go back to the CIA again. She wasn't that person anymore.

She'd find out the truth behind David's death, because the stakes had never been greater. Failure wasn't an option because it could mean tragedy for this innocent family. She'd do whatever was necessary to bring down these men, even if came at the greatest cost—her life.

Victoria's pretty features twisted into a frown. Aaron believed she was working out the best way to return to the cabin. She'd want him to stay behind for his own protection, but he couldn't do that. No matter what, he wouldn't let her go there by herself.

Aaron slipped into the chair beside her and she turned, her gaze drawn to his injury. "Let me have a look at that. I'll see if your mother has something to clean it." She rose and went to the kitchen while he tried to picture what she must have been like as a young Amish girl. He could almost see her smiling and carefree, holding her *mamm's* hand.

Victoria came back carrying a wet cloth and some bandages and he pushed aside those thoughts.

She gently tore away a portion of his shirt to reveal the bullet wound and leaned in close to inspect the damage. He tensed and became aware of each little breath she took. This woman had a way of breaking down the walls he'd built around his heart. She inched her way into his life, and he wasn't sure how he felt about it.

"The bullet passed clean through," she said, and glanced at his face. "It's not serious."

Aaron managed a nod and kept his attention on the fire while she did her best to clean the wound. Once finished, she covered it with a bandage.

"Let me have a look at the back of your head. You hit that rock pretty hard." She gently examined the place where he fallen against the rock. A nasty knot had popped up that hurt terribly. "It's not so bad," she assured him once she'd finished cleaning away the caked blood. "But you should take it easy in case you have a concussion."

When she would have moved away, he grabbed her hand to keep her there. "Whatever you are thinking about doing, don't." In her eyes, he saw things she didn't want him to.

Victoria blew out a heavy sigh and slipped out of his grip into the chair beside him.

"Aaron, this has gone way beyond me getting the evidence from the cabin. I've put you and your entire family in danger. These men are deadly serious. They will let nothing stand in their way."

He didn't look away. "It doesn't matter."

She ran a hand through the tangles in her hair. "It does. I won't let you put yourself in harm's way again. Think about Caleb. You saw how terrified he was. What if he lost you?"

Aaron never broke eye contact. "What kind of example would I be setting for Caleb if I left you to fend for yourself? I *am* thinking about my *sohn*."

"And what if those men come back?" She searched his face and waited for him to say something.

Without a doubt, there was a real chance that might happen. "I'm going to send my family to stay with a friend for a while. Jonah and his *fraa* live some ways from here. They will be safe there." He glanced over to where his brothers were talking, near the kitchen. "Stay here where it's warm."

He stood. As he went over to them, he looked back at Victoria. She hung her head. He couldn't imagine the guilt she was experiencing, but he wanted her to understand none of it was her fault. She was just another innocent victim.

"What do you wish to do? I don't think it's safe for *Mamm* and Caleb to stay here." Fletcher wore a worried frown on his face.

"You're right, it's not. I think you and Hunter should take them to Jonah's for a while. You'll have to take the back way. I just hope those men don't hear you leaving and try to follow." Aaron glanced between his brothers and saw the same troubled reaction from both.

"We'll be as quiet as possible. What about you and Victoria?" Hunter looked past him to Victoria. "You can't go back to that cabin. It's too dangerous."

Aaron sighed. "I don't have a choice. The information there is too important to leave for these men to find." He hesitated. "Please, *bruders*, I need you to do this for me. I don't want to be worried about them or you."

Fletcher and Hunter exchanged a look before agreeing.

"*Oke*, we'll do as you wish," Fletcher told him.

Aaron forced a smile. "*Denki*. But you must hurry in case those men decide to return."

While his brothers went to harness the wagon as quietly as possible, he found his mother in the kitchen with Caleb and told them both what he had planned.

"I want to go with you, *Daed*." Caleb said with fresh tears hovering in his eyes. The boy had been terrified ever since they'd found Victoria in the building.

Aaron kneeled in front of Caleb. "You can't, *sohn*, because it's too dangerous. And I need you to look after your *grossmammi*. As soon as I am able, I'll come get you." Aaron looked to his *mamm*. "Get together what you need for the trip."

She nodded and hurried away. His mother kept a few of her things here at Hunter's for when she stayed from time to time.

The boy's tears spilled down his cheeks, and he swiped them away with the back of his hand. "But you could get hurt. These men have guns." Caleb's bottom lip trembled.

Aaron clasped his *sohn's* shoulders and looked him in the eye. "Yes, but we will be careful. You do not have to worry. Go with your *onkels* and your *grossmammi*. I will be fine."

Caleb scrubbed his eyes once more and wrapped his arms around his father's neck.

The love in Aaron's heart for this boy went beyond measure. He'd protect Caleb even if it meant giving up his own life.

He held the boy close for a moment longer,

then untangled Caleb's arms from around his neck. "Be strong for your *grossmammi*."

"O-oke," the boy responded, gulping out his answer.

Aaron helped his *sohn* into his coat, then put his on and waited by the back door until his mother returned.

"Ready?" he asked, and she nodded. Together, they stepped outside.

Fletcher had the wagon ready and parked around the back of the house. He and Hunter hopped down and came up the steps.

Aaron nodded to Fletcher, who took Caleb by the hand while Hunter guided their *mamm* down the steps to the waiting wagon.

Once his mother and *sohn* were in the wagon, Aaron pulled aside his brothers. "You have your shotgun?" he whispered to Hunter.

"Jah. Thankfully, those men down the path didn't appear to have heard us bringing out the wagon," Hunter said.

Still, Aaron didn't want to take any chances. "Keep the weapon with you and keep to the pastures until you reach Jonah's home," he said in a low voice.

"We will." Hunter glanced around in the darkness. "We should go. Stay safe and protect her, brother."

Aaron hugged both brothers and stepped

back. He watched as Fletcher eased the wagon past the house in the same direction he and Victoria had taken.

"Please keep them safe," he prayed earnestly before he stepped back inside.

Victoria looked up as he entered the living room.

Aaron reclaimed his chair beside her and laid the handgun he'd shoved inside his pocket across his leg. "They will be *oke*. Caleb is worried, but he is a strong boy. He will be fine."

"He loves you so much," she said softly. "He can't lose you, as well. Believe me, I know what it's like to lose both your parents." She stopped and stared at him, her eyes troubled.

"You must have been young when your father passed. What happened to him?" He watched her face and saw the all-too-familiar emotions he carried, too. Grief. Guilt. So many more were carved on her face.

"He died when I was but a toddler. My mother said it was an accident, but she never really told me how." She glanced up and saw his surprise. "It was just me and my mother for several years. She was my world." A smile hovered on her lips.

"What happened to your *mamm*?"

She clenched her hands into fists. After all these years, he sensed it was hard to speak about her mother.

"The doctor said it was pneumonia. *Mamm* didn't want me to see how ill she was." She swallowed several times while he thought about how closely her story resembled his. Irene hadn't wanted him to know, either.

"My mother worked at an Amish-owned bakery and I went with her to work. I loved her so much, and I loved being Amish. And then she got sick."

The pain on her face broke his heart.

"I found her one morning. She wasn't conscious. I didn't know what to do, so I ran to the neighbor's home and told them. The husband went to call an ambulance while the wife brought me home." She stopped for a moment to collect herself. "My mother was in the hospital for a week, then she died."

Aaron couldn't imagine how hard it had been for such a young child to understand death.

"You went to live with your cousin then?"

She looked at him. "Yes. There were no living family members among the community, but I had a distant cousin in Michigan who wasn't Amish. I stayed with the neighbors until they arrived and took me home with them." She shook her head. "I cried for months afterward missing my *mamm*. I hated living with my cousin and her husband. They were much older and had no children of their own. Though they did their best, they had little patience for a young girl. I thought my life had ended." She pulled in several breaths. He wondered if she even realized she'd used the Pennsylvania Dutch word for mother.

"In time, I adjusted. Grew up. Went away to college and later was recruited by the CIA. I joined because I thought I could so some good." She shook her head. "But I ended up losing my compass. Through the things I did in life—all the dangerous missions—I never forgot my simple childhood. Never stopped longing for it."

"You didn't try to return to the faith?" he asked quietly, and she glanced at him.

"I've done things, Aaron. Terrible things. I'm not worthy of being Amish anymore."

The catch in her voice tore at his heart. "I don't believe that's so." When she didn't respond, he asked, "And your cousin and her husband? Do they know you're here?" He was curious about the couple who raised her.

"They passed when I was in college. I have no one left." She sounded so sad. Victoria had come so far from the Plain world, but it wasn't her fault.

Aaron reached for her hand and held it. "It's not too late. You left before you were of age to join the church. You can come back."

He scarcely knew her, and yet he'd found

himself drawn to Victoria from the moment they met. He'd gone against his own upbringing so that she could find out who killed her partner. What if these men were successful and they killed her? The thought was terrifying. She'd fought so hard—survived things most people never dealt with—to live. She deserved to be happy. If that meant returning to the Amish way of life, then so be it.

But what if he couldn't keep her safe? What if he couldn't protect his family? If they all died trying to find the people responsible for David's death, then these men would walk away free and clear.

Anger boiled up inside of him. No matter what, he wouldn't let that happen. Because Victoria's fight had become his.

"We should get out of here while we still can," she said in a spent voice. Dredging up her troubled past seemed to have taken a toll. "Somehow, these men keep finding me and it's best if we don't stay in one place for long. I think they may have tracked my phone somehow through my former commander."

He raised his eyebrows. "How do you suppose they were able to do that?" The vast amount of technology available to these men was way beyond his understanding.

"My guess is they would know of my friendship with Robert and would be monitoring his calls, expecting me to reach out to him. And they were correct. I did."

"Why are you so sure these men are from your former employer?" This was what he didn't understand. Her people were supposed to be the good guys.

"Because of David," she said with a sigh, then told him about her partner's final warning. "They're CIA, I'm positive."

If someone as prepared for this as Victoria was worried, then he had no idea what they were up against. "I've searched through all of my possessions," she said. "There's no tracking device planted on anything. The only explanation is they traced my calls to Robert. I spoke to him after I arrived here in West Kootenai. If that's the case, I can't afford to use this phone to contact him. It's too dangerous. I'll have to destroy it."

She looked around the room. "I left it here when we went back to the cabin earlier." Victoria rose and went into the kitchen.

The ways of this intelligence community seemed underhanded to Aaron.

Victoria brought her phone over and removed the battery. She opened the glass door to the woodstove and tossed the phone inside, leaving the battery on the kitchen table.

"As soon as I'm able, I must find a way to warn Robert he could be in danger."

A log in the woodstove rolled off the top, sending sparks flying, startling her.

Outside, something unusual caught his attention. Aaron bolted from his seat. "Did you hear that?"

"I did." Victoria rushed to the front window and inched the curtain apart, searching the darkness outside.

"There are lights in the woods. They're coming in on foot. From the looks of it, there's more than just two people out there." Victoria jumped away from the window. "We'll have to go out the back." She grabbed the cloak and fastened it around her shoulders. Though the garment was warm, it wouldn't provide the protection needed to survive the bitter cold.

"Here, take this." Aaron handed her Hunter's extra jacket from where it hung by the door.

They couldn't afford to take a lantern for light. "Hunter keeps several flashlights in the kitchen for emergencies, though we won't be able to use the light for a while." Aaron grabbed one.

Victoria peered out the window once more. "They're getting closer."

Aaron ran to the back door and cracked it. "I don't see anyone." Still, stepping out onto the porch was a hard thing to do. His hands shook as Victoria followed him out. Nothing but silence surrounded them. As they got ready to leave the porch, a noise at the side of the house grabbed Aaron's attention. It sounded like a twig snapping beneath someone's foot.

They were out of time.

"Make a run for it." Victoria grabbed his hand. Together they ran from the porch toward the nearby woods.

They'd covered but a few steps when the world around them erupted in gunfire. Shots came from both sides of the house. Surrounded, their only option was to keep running.

NINE

"Get down as low as you can!" Victoria said and ducked as another round of shots whizzed past them. Still holding hands, they were almost to the trees when more gunfire erupted.

She pushed Aaron into the woods and fired back toward the barrel flashes. "Keep going. I'll be right behind you."

A stray bullet struck the Glock, and the vibration from the shot forced the gun from her hand. She'd lost her only means of protecting herself.

Victoria dropped to her knees. With her hands spread out in front of her, she frantically searched the snowy ground for the Glock.

She could hear them advancing on her location. Her hand connected with the gun. Not much time. The men were almost on top of her now.

She jerked the weapon toward the men, but before she fired a single round, a shot from behind her flew past her head. Aaron had her back.

Victoria opened fire, as well. The men dove for cover.

"Go, go, go." She stumbled to her feet. Aaron grabbed her arm and together they ran.

"They know we're here now. Whatever you do, don't stop. Even if I can't make it, keep going."

He'd never let her go. "That's not happening."

It was pointless to argue. She'd deal with the situation if it arose. Aaron was an honorable man who would give his life for hers.

"We can't outrun them. Find someplace to get out of sight." Victoria searched around in the darkness. "There." A tree appeared to have been struck by lightning and had snapped into two pieces.

Slipping behind the damaged tree, she and Aaron crouched low while she prayed for God's protection to keep them hidden from the enemy.

"They can't have gone far. I'm pretty sure I hit her," a familiar voice said. Not Logan, but one of the men from the woods earlier.

Victoria instinctively moved closer to Aaron in a protective gesture. She'd fight to the death to keep him safe.

"They're not here. Let's keep moving. He's determined they don't walk out of here alive." Those chilling words settled around Victoria. Who was this man they spoke of?

After a moment, their footsteps faded. Aaron peeked from behind the tree. "I don't see them." He stood and held out his hand for her. "There could be others coming after them. We should change directions."

"That's smart. Which way?" she asked while trying to get her bearings. They were somewhere behind Hunter's home, but in the dark, it was hard to tell exactly where they were.

He glanced around before pointing to the left of the downed tree. "This way. It will take us longer to reach your cabin, but at least we'll be hidden by the woods and not out in the open."

Snow continued to fall harder as they walked. All she could think about was the possibility that these men were watching Robert, as well. Somehow, she had to find a way to warn him that he could be in danger.

Soon, the trees thinned. A clearing separated the woods from a house. They stopped for a breath and to listen.

"Which way from here?" They couldn't afford to make one false move.

"To your right," he said, and they began walking again. The best way to fight the cold.

Fat snowflakes fell harder, covering them in white and muting the world around them. It was an idyllic setting, but the situation they faced was anything but ideal.

A road appeared in front of them. "What do we do now? We can't afford to be seen on the road."

Aaron stopped beside her. "Trust me, Victoria. I won't put us in danger, I promise."

Facing life-and-death decisions had allowed her to get to know Aaron quickly. Like her, he'd lost so much. Everything he did and said confirmed what she'd believed from the beginning. He was a good man.

She didn't hesitate. "I trust you completely."

He smiled at her answer. "There's a shortcut a little ways down this road. Hunter and I use it a lot when traveling between our homes. It's rarely used by others from the community, and for sure no one outside would know of its existence. We'll be safe."

Safe. The idea was something that remained elusive. She longed for it, had searched desperately to obtain that sense of safety since David's passing, but at this point, Victoria wondered if she would ever feel safe again.

Nothing but their ragged breathing and muffled footsteps could be heard in the night, yet Aaron was unable to relax. These men were smart, and they knew he and Victoria were hiding somewhere within the community. They'd search every single house, barn and shed.

"You're positive you didn't recognize any of those men back there from your past?" he asked again. Reason suggested she'd know at least one of them.

Victoria rousted herself from her own troubled thoughts. "I know what you're thinking, but no."

"Maybe they're not CIA? Maybe this isn't connected to your former employer at all."

"I almost wish I could believe that," she said in a quiet voice. "To think that our own people killed David…" She sighed deeply. "I can't imagine the betrayal he must have experienced."

Aaron struggled to keep his frustration from getting the better of him. "But you're sure these men are CIA?"

She didn't hesitate. "Without a doubt. They're dirty agents, and they killed David and the rest of our team to cover up their crimes. Something has them convinced I have evidence to tie them to their crimes."

He recalled what Logan had said about someone not being happy. "It appears there's someone else above this Logan fellow who's really in control."

"I agree. The question is who?"

"We'll figure it out." He stopped walking and touched her face. Felt her lean into his hand for a moment.

"It's been a year, Aaron, and I'm no closer to understanding what happened than I was that day David died. I thought once I looked through the information he'd gathered, it would all make sense, but so far, all I have are more questions."

"The answers will come to you," he whispered and believed it. More than anything, he wanted her to have another chance at happiness. Whether here among the Amish, or someplace else, she deserved to be happy.

Victoria looked deep into his eyes. The woman standing before him was beautiful and she made him wish for things that could never be.

With a sad heart, he let his hand drop and started walking again. Irene had been the love of his life. They'd known each other since they were *kinner*. How could he think about another woman when his wife's death was all his fault?

Aaron spotted the path he was looking for. There was just enough room to take a buggy through, but certainly not a car. Still, he couldn't relax. It was impossible not to react to every little noise. Anyone listening carefully would hear their approach. Aaron tried not to think about what happened the last time they'd gone to the cabin. Victoria had almost died.

He glanced at her face profiled in the darkness. Her hair was loose around her shoulders.

Dressed in Hunter's oversize coat, she hunched against the cold and the months of running that had piled up on her.

"The woods around the cabin are thick. We should have plenty of coverage." She looked his way. "I hope it's enough."

Aaron understood what she wasn't saying. It was just the two of them. They'd need all the help they could get.

He checked his handgun. "I'm almost out of bullets." The weapon wouldn't be much good if they were forced into another shoot-out.

Victoria scrubbed her hand over her eyes. "I'm almost empty, too. Let's hope we don't have to engage them."

Doubts continued to plague Aaron. They'd been this close to the cabin before. Would this trip end in the same disaster as the previous one? Or worse?

Please, Gott, *keep us safe. Let us find the evidence.*

Though the darkness covered their presence, there could be no concealing their footprints if anyone should look close enough.

Up ahead, the cabin appeared through the trees, a dark mass in the snow-covered world. As they edged closer, Aaron noticed two men guarding the place. One was stationed at the back of the cabin and a second near the entrance. Were there others?

"I'll draw the men away from the entrance. That will give you time to get the box and get out of there as fast as possible."

She stopped him. "No, Aaron. Watch the man at the back. I'll get past the guy in the front." She stepped forward and placed a gentle kiss on his cheek. "Stay safe."

When she would have pulled away, he reached for her hand and kept her close. More than anything, he wished he could give her back the childhood she'd lost, the life she longed for, but he couldn't.

"Be careful," he said instead of what he wanted to say. *I care about you. I don't want anything to happen to you. Please be safe.*

She was inches from him, close enough for him to feel her breath on his cheek. She touched his face. "I will. Don't you let anything happen to you." The roughness in her tone made him focus harder. There were things she wasn't saying, either. Perhaps it was best this way.

With another searching look, she disappeared into the trees near the front of the house. And all he could think about was everything he might lose here tonight.

TEN

The man standing guard was smoking a cigarette. Its tip glowed through the continuous fall of snowflakes.

Just a few more steps and she would be able to reach him. Hopefully, she could take him out of commission quickly and get the evidence before the second man got wind. Yet all she could think about was Aaron. She cared about him—couldn't deny it—but she had to stay focused. Both their lives depended on it.

The man at the front of the cabin stepped away from the door. Had he heard her? The noise of her heartbeat was the only sound around. She held her breath as he came to within a few feet.

The waft of cigarette smoke hit her. He leaned into the woods close to where she stood. This was it.

Victoria grabbed him before he had time to run. Though she had the element of surprise, his strength was far superior to hers in this weakened state. He freed himself and slugged her jaw hard. Pain rippled from the contact point and she stumbled backward. Before she could set her feet and square off, he was on top of her.

He grabbed a handful of her hair and prepared to strike her again. Victoria kicked him hard in the shin. He screamed in pain and let her go. She had no doubt his partner could hear their struggle and would come to his aid soon enough.

With a guttural growl, she grabbed hold of the man's neck and squeezed hard. Bringing down a full-grown man in her depleted condition wouldn't be easy. He fought like a wild animal, kicking and pummeling her. Through it all, Victoria held on. Eventually, his efforts subsided, and he slumped against her. She dropped to her knees and managed to shove him free. Resting her hands on her knees, she sucked in air.

"Are you okay, Hal?" the second man called out. She wouldn't be able to get inside the cabin until he was subdued.

She started for the back of the cabin. Before she reached him, noises of a scuffle could be heard. Aaron! She ran faster.

Victoria rounded the back of the cabin. The man had Aaron in a choke hold. She didn't hesitate. She charged the man and slammed her Glock against the back of his head. He immediately freed Aaron and fell backward.

"You saved my life," Aaron murmured, still shaken from the encounter.

She grabbed his hand. "Let's get the box and leave before these two wake up. There could be others on the way here now." The threat facing them was endless.

At the front of the cabin, Victoria slowly opened the door. What if there were more men inside? The thought was crippling.

Her heart sank when she entered the cabin. It had been ransacked. Victoria ran to her hiding spot in the living room and dropped to her knees. Her fingers shook as she pried the boards free. The box was where she'd left it.

She sat back on her heels. "Thank You, God." Grabbing it, she headed for the door, where Aaron was waiting.

Even if she figured out what David was trying to tell her, without her burner phone, she would have no way of reaching the one person from her CIA past she still trusted. Which meant she'd have to find another way to contact Robert. For now, they had to stay alive long enough to go through the evidence again. One problem at a time.

With Aaron behind her, Victoria cracked

open the door a sliver. All they had to do was reach the woods. Before she could slip out of the house a sound nearby threatened to take away all hope. The voices of more than one person were coming their way.

She closed the door and raced back to the kitchen. Several men approached the cabin. Once they saw the two unconscious men, they'd know she was there. Which left only one way out.

"Come with me," she whispered to Aaron.

Inside the bedroom, the window was still open from the last time she'd crawled through it. She had the advantage this time. The men didn't know she and Aaron were there. Yet.

Victoria handed the metal box to Aaron and jumped on the bed and slipped through the window while carefully protecting her injured leg.

Aaron tossed the box down to her before he came through and dropped to the ground. Once he was beside her, they ran for the trees. They reached the first group just as the men passed by. So far, they were unaware of their unconscious colleagues. That wouldn't last long.

"We have to take care of her and the man before they get someone to listen to them. When that happens, there will be no containing this, and he's expecting an update within the hour."

Goose bumps sped up Victoria's arms. She

clutched the metal box tight and prayed the answers were in there somewhere, because her bad feeling had continued to grow. It screamed she and Aaron were running out of time. It wouldn't matter what the evidence pointed to if they were caught. She and Aaron would both be dead.

After the last man passed, Aaron let himself breathe normally again. He turned to leave with Victoria.

"We've got a man down. They've been here!"

"Hurry, Aaron." Victoria ran as fast as she could.

"I see them! They're getting away!" another man yelled.

Victoria didn't slow down, and Aaron struggled to keep up with her pace. They were approaching the base of the mountain. If trapped here, it wouldn't end well for them.

At the rate the men were coming after them, they'd never get away on foot.

Aaron struggled to recall what he remembered about the mountain. He and his brothers had explored every square inch of it growing up. They'd discovered a bunch of tunnels running through it. If he and Victoria could reach one of the entrances without being spotted, they had a chance. His knowledge of the tunnels would give them an advantage.

"Follow me. I know a way out." Aaron quickly took the lead.

Victoria glanced behind them. "They're coming up fast." The words had just cleared her lips when the men reinforced their presence with gunfire.

Aaron ducked low and ran with Victoria on his heels.

The rugged rock wall came up fast. He prayed he remembered where the entrance was after so many years.

More bullets flew past them.

"Which way?" The edge in Victoria's voice confirmed the urgency.

He squinted through the continuous snowfall. "There!" As he headed for what he hoped was the tunnel's entrance, Victoria fired off a shot to force the men to take cover. With their limited ammunition, they couldn't afford to waste bullets.

He remembered the opening was hidden behind a large boulder near the mountainside. When he found what he believed was the rock, he slipped behind it. The tunnel opening appeared covered in overgrowth. He knees went weak when he realized this was his childhood haunt.

Aaron shoved aside a small pine tree that had sprouted near the entrance and went inside with

Victoria. A silty twilight pressed in on them immediately.

"Which way from here? It won't take them long to find the opening."

Aaron's memory came back quickly. He moved toward the one path that would bring them out on the other side of the mountain. It wasn't a direct route, which would work in their favor.

Voices echoed off the walls behind them. The shooters had found the entrance.

"Are you sure this is the right way?" Victoria asked after he made a wrong turn and they were forced to backtrack. "We can't afford any more mistakes."

"This is it," he said with confidence, positive they were on the right track.

He kept up a quick pace down the narrow passage that was scarcely wide enough for the two of them to walk beside each other.

"Where does this end up?" Victoria asked between labored breaths, so Aaron slowed his speed.

"After some ways, it lets out on the other side of the mountain, beyond the Amish community. I have an *Englisch* friend who owns a ranch over there. He will help us, and he has a phone you can use to call your former commander."

The relief on her face was worth any amount of trouble they'd face.

His brothers and Aaron used to come here whenever their work allowed them the free time growing up. They'd explored each passage and played hide-and-seek in here all the time. How many times in recent years had he wished for some of those good moments back?

Thinking about the rift that had separated his brothers Mason and Eli after both became interested in the same young woman still stung. The family never had recovered from the damage.

He glanced at Victoria. His family's troubles were nothing compared to hers. Losing her mother so young was unimaginable. A little girl needed her *mamm*. She must have felt so lost being forced into a different way of life. He'd give anything to be able to take away all her pain, make her life happy again.

He wished he could make himself happy, too. He hadn't been since Irene's passing, but if he was honest, the tragedies his family had suffered had dimmed his happiness long before that.

Despite the threat to their lives, there was one blessing to come from facing these terrible men. It showed him what was important in life. Living with the guilt of his neglect was wrong, and

Irene would not have wished for him to continue to blame himself. She'd want him to be happy.

Something about Victoria stirred his heart. His feelings toward her were changing. But she was caught up in her own guilt. At some point, she'd have to let go of it and find her way into whatever the future held. Aaron had to do the same, and he was ready. So ready. Carrying the burden of guilt for so long was exhausting. He wanted a chance to live.

ELEVEN

Exhaustion weighed down her limbs, yet they had to keep moving. Putting distance between themselves and the threat following them was critical.

Once they were a safe way from the entrance, Aaron clicked on the flashlight he'd brought from Hunter's home.

"We can rest for a bit if you'd like," he whispered and dropped to the ground. She sat beside him.

"They'll check every single passage in this mountain. Eventually, they'll find this one. We probably shouldn't rest for long," she said with a hint of regret.

He reached for her hand when she would have stood. "Catch your breath for a second." He indicated the box in her hand and kept his voice low. "You said there was more than the photos of the truck?"

Victoria gathered a breath and tried to relax.

They hadn't heard any sounds from the tunnels in a long time. She wondered if the men were still back there somewhere. "Yes. There are a couple of pictures of what appears to be a meeting in the desert. David must have taken them from a distance because it's hard to make out much about the people gathered there. All are dressed in dark clothing and facing away from the camera." She kept her voice low as she told him about the photo of the ledger. "I know those numbers mean something important, but for the life of me I don't understand what."

"When we get to my friend's place and you have a chance to look through them again, I'm sure it will begin to make sense." He rose and held out his hand to her.

More than anything she wanted to believe him. So much was riding on her figuring out the meaning before those men shut her down.

Victoria clasped his hand and let him pull her to her feet. Mere inches separated them. He'd gone against so many things in his faith in to assist her. He'd put his life and his family's in jeopardy. All because he believed in her.

Coming close to death solidified the decision in her mind. If she survived this, she was done with the spy world. She'd seen enough death and danger to last a lifetime. More than anything she longed for the simple life she'd once been part of. And she'd do whatever necessary to come back to her Amish roots one day.

Looking at Aaron, she knew her feelings for him were growing and had been for a little while. Caring was turning into something far stronger. More than anything she wished it were possible to simply wipe the slate clean of all the bad things she's done in the past and stay here in West Kootenai to become part of the community. Would it be possible for two wounded souls to find happiness together? She couldn't let herself have that hope. Not with the truth behind David's death still hanging over her head. Not with dozens of men trying to end both their existences.

"We should keep going." The rough edge to his voice made her focus harder on his face. When he looked at her, Aaron only saw good. Her past didn't matter to him. If only it didn't matter to her.

She touched his face. No matter what the outcome, she owed him her life. "You're right, we should keep going." But she didn't move. She wanted to stay here with him a little longer. Danger waited outside the walls of this tunnel.

He reached for her hand and held it for a moment. A tender smile replaced the serious expression he'd worn. He let her go. The moment passed.

They started down the narrow passage once again. How long had they been inside the mountain? Hours at least. By the time they reached Aaron's friends, it would be almost daylight. They'd be exposed.

Aaron grabbed hold of her arm and Victoria stopped and looked at him. "What's wrong?"

"Nothing. Listen."

She did. "Is that?"

"*Jah*, the wind. We're at the exit."

Victoria had never been so happy to be facing the cold as she was right now.

As they reached the opening, the wind howled around the side of the mountain, shutting out all other sounds. They couldn't afford to take any chances.

At this point, the entire community was saturated with enemy soldiers. They could have people watching this side of the mountain.

"Wait here for a second. Let me make sure it's safe to go outside."

He grabbed her arm. "I'm going with you." The set of his jaw confirmed he would go whether she wanted him to or not. "We are in this together. Where you go, I go." What he said reminded her of a favorite bible verse in the Book of Ruth and she smiled.

"Okay, but stay close. I'm worried about what we'll find out there."

They stepped out into the storm that had grown in intensity during their time in the mountain. It was hard to see a few feet in front of them.

"How far to your friend's place?" she asked when they'd been at it for a while and hadn't made much progress. The driving wind came right at them.

"A couple of miles. Maybe more."

"We won't be able to cover much ground under these conditions." As they stopped to rest, Victoria looked around for a place to take shelter, but there was nothing but the wind and snow.

It felt as if each time they had a glimmer of hope, something came along to snatch it away.

The storm continued to rage. They wouldn't last long like this. The temperature was well below freezing, and the driving snow had soaked their clothes. They should have waited out the storm in the tunnel and took their chances with the men stumbling upon the exit. This was all his fault. He'd thought they could make it to Ethan's place. He'd risked both their lives. After everything Victoria had been through, if he let her die out here from exposure, he'd never forgive himself.

Aaron looked around and tried to recall the layout of the land. Many old miners' cabins were still standing and scattered along this side of the mountain. If they could make it to one of them, perhaps they could wait out the storm in the shelter of the cabin.

The last time he and his brothers had been here, most of the cabins were falling apart from years of Montana winters. What must they be like now?

"We'll never make it to my friend's home in these conditions." He told her about the abandoned cabins. "If we reach one, we could get out of the weather at least to wait out the storm. Hopefully, it will be moving out soon."

"Sounds perfect right about now. Lead the way."

Squinting through the thick snow, he reclaimed his bearings and headed off to the right.

Victoria fell into step beside him. She braced herself against the brutal wind that seemed to cut right through them. Staying upright was hard.

Once they entered the wilderness, the trees gave some relief from the driving wind.

Aaron's doubts returned in full force. Was this the right way? It had been several years since he'd been here last, and the landscape had changed. What if he had them wandering around in the freezing weather, possibly to their deaths?

They trudged through the deep snow that had gathered in drifts up to several feet high around the trees.

"At least it's not as cold in here," Victoria said and forced a smile.

Beyond his labored breathing, a sound put Aaron on edge. He stopped suddenly when he realized they were not the only ones in the woods.

Victoria heard it, too, and pulled him behind a tree.

"I don't believe they came this way." Aaron recognized Logan's voice right away. "They're probably still hiding inside the mountain. You two, stay here just in case. Alert us if you see them. The rest of you come with me. We're going back to the entrance to the tunnels."

Aaron's gaze latched on to Victoria's face. She was listening intently. The men were close enough that they could hear their panicked breathing.

"Let's get a move on," Logan exclaimed with anger in his voice. "They won't survive long in these conditions if they're out in the open. Still,

I want them found, one way or another. Get me proof they're dead. Do it quickly."

Their footsteps tramped away. Several minutes passed before Aaron chanced a look around the tree where he and Victoria had taken cover. Two men remained close.

As he ducked back behind the tree, his foot connected with a tree branch on the ground. It snapped beneath his weight and he froze. His frantic eyes held Victoria's.

"Did you hear that?" A second passed, then the same man said, "Go. Check it out. I don't want to have to explain to *him* why we let them get away again. I'm not ready to die for this."

Aaron's eyes widened. Would these men turn on each other? The man certainly sounded worried.

We have to leave, he mouthed, but Victoria shook her head.

"All right, I'm going," the man grumbled and tramped through the snow.

Aaron tensed as a set of heavy footsteps came closer. A man's labored breathing stopped on the other side of the tree.

They must have made some sound because the man jerked toward them. Victoria grabbed him before he could react and pulled him toward her and out of the other man's view. She clamped her hand over his mouth to keep him from calling out to his partner. He struggled in her grasp, but she didn't let up. After what felt like an eternity, the man's eyes rolled back in his head as he lost consciousness. Victoria lowered him to the ground.

"What's going on over there, Carl?" the second person demanded. A moment of silence was followed by the man trudging through the snow. There would be no disguising the unconscious man.

The man stopped when he spotted Carl and pointed his gun out in front of him.

Victoria didn't hesitate. She jumped from behind the tree, taking the man by surprise. Before he could manage a single shot, she had him by the throat and was choking him hard. The man thrashed around as he struggled to free himself, but Victoria stood her ground and continued to cut off his air supply.

When he went limp, she slowly laid him on the ground. "Grab their weapons. We need to put as much space as we can between us and them."

Aaron retrieved both guns and stuck them in his pockets while she destroyed their phones. "We can't risk having them call for help, and there's a good chance the phones can be tracked."

All he could think about was how close they'd

both come to dying. How many more chances would they get?

He forced himself to stay focused. Reaching the cabins was critical now.

Victoria glanced up at the sky through the trees. If anything, the storm appeared to be increasing in strength. "This new snowfall will cover our tracks and they'll have to hike back around the mountain to reach their buddies. It should buy us some time."

Aaron didn't answer. All he could think about was the distance between them and safety. He wondered what would be their worst challenge—the weather, or men with everything to lose.

TWELVE

Thick snow continued to fall from the sky. It was impossible to see more than a few inches in front of them. Victoria looked back in the direction they'd come, but the landscape behind them had disappeared into a sea of white. The deluge of snow covered them and their footprints. There was no way the men coming after them had the means to track her physically. At this point, it was just a matter of staying hidden and finding a way to reach Robert. They'd need his help to get out of this mess.

Aaron grabbed her arm. "I see the cabin." He pointed straight ahead. Victoria couldn't see anything.

"What am I looking at?" She squinted through the thick snowfall.

"There's a cabin over that ridge." Aaron moved past her to what appeared to be a snowdrift.

She reached his side just as he was trying to

shove open the door. Victoria squeezed in beside him and placed her shoulder against the wooden door to assist. It took several tries before it budged.

Together, they stumbled inside a one-room cabin that hadn't been used in years. Aaron shined the flashlight around. Dust coated the few pieces of furniture. Against one wall, a rudimentary fireplace still stood intact. The last occupant had piled wood nearby. She couldn't imagine how many years it had been there. Starting a fire would be a risk, but they were both facing life or death now. They were both soaking wet. It wouldn't take long for hypothermia to set in.

"We have to warm up or we won't make it much farther," she told him. "The temperature here is only slightly warmer than outside and we're both in danger of succumbing to the cold. We have to start a fire."

"You're right. And with a storm this intense, spotting white smoke among all the snow and clouds will be nearly impossible." Aaron pointed to the fireplace. "There's wood. It doesn't appear to be damp. Let's hope there are matches." He went over to the mantel and searched it before turning to her. "Nothing."

Victoria glanced down at the box in her hand. It contained the photos, David's destroyed cell phone that she'd taken the battery out of long ago…and his grandfather's lighter. David always carried his grandfather's lighter with him in memory of the man he loved who had fought in the Second World War.

She opened the box and brought out the tool. Was it even in working order? David never used it.

"Here, let's try this." She held up the lighter.

Aaron searched for something to use as kindling and found an old newspaper that had probably been left for that purpose. He stacked wood onto the fireplace grate and then crumpled up paper to ignite the wood.

The flashlight's beam caught the lighter in her hand. Victoria shook it. It sounded like there was still some fluid inside. Would it be enough?

The striker rolled across the flint. Nothing happened.

"Let me have a try." Aaron took it from her, tore off a piece of paper and held it up next to the lighter. It took three attempts before it ignited. He stuck the paper against the flame, and it caught quickly. He touched the lit paper against the other pieces in the fireplace. Soon, the wood ignited, and the fire grew.

Heat permeated the space in front of the fireplace. Victoria stood close and warmed her hands. "I never thought something as simple as a fire would feel this nice."

Aaron chuckled. "Me, neither. I've made hundreds of fires in my life, but none have felt this *gut* before."

She looked at him with admiration. He'd never once faltered through all they'd gone through. Victoria squeezed his arm and smiled. "I'm so sorry for all of this."

"You have nothing to be sorry for," he assured her. The sincerity on his face confirmed he believed only good things about her. But he didn't know the truth.

As he cupped her chin, the firelight caught the gentling in his eyes, and she closed hers. This moment would live in her memory forever.

Since that last Christmas with her mother, even though her adopted parents had done their best, she'd been searching her entire life to recapture the special feeling of the season that she'd had among her Amish people. Many of her recent Christmases had been spent in other countries. She and David had celebrated a few together, but nothing came close to the simple moments from her past.

Aaron reminded her of that time, of the things that were important and what she wanted so desperately. Was it possible to come back to this way of life?

She clasped his hand, brought it against her lips and kissed his palm before she let him go. All the wishes in her heart would have to wait. She had unfinished business. Her life and her heart were stuck in Neutral. Until she found the people who killed David and knew the real reason why he'd died, there was no moving on.

Victoria turned toward the fire. "The wind's settling. I think the brunt of the storm is passing. Once we thaw out, we should keep moving."

He didn't say a word for the longest time. She glanced at him. If only she understood the meaning behind his set jaw, gathered eyebrows and clenched hands.

"You're right," he murmured. "But after what we've gone through so far, I think we both could use a few more minutes of warmth."

She smiled despite her heavy heart. "Yes, we could."

He stepped closer to the fire and next to her. "You are a good person, Victoria, and you didn't deserve any of what's happened to you."

She'd give everything for that to be true, but Aaron didn't know the things she'd done, the lives she'd taken and the cost to her soul.

"It doesn't matter," he said softly, as if reading her thoughts. "No matter what happened in your past, I see you are a good person. So does *Gott*."

She swallowed several times. If only she saw herself the way he did.

Aaron turned her to face him. A breath of space separated them. "*Gott* sees the heart. Not what we are sometimes forced to do. He has forgiven you. It's time you learned to forgive yourself."

Was it as simple as that? A sob escaped and the tears she'd kept hidden for so long refused to hide any longer.

He tugged her into his arms, and she held him tight. The steady beat of his heart against her ear was the best sound ever.

What she'd left behind her was as unresolved as what stood in front. More than ever, Victoria was determined she would do whatever possible to bring Aaron through this nightmare unscathed.

"Who owns this cabin?" she asked, content to stay in his arms for as long as possible.

"My friend. He owns most of the land on this side. He is a *gut* customer, as well. Ethan has bought many of my pieces for his home."

"He sounds like a nice person," she said, and reluctantly pulled away.

Aaron scraped back hair from her face. "He is. I'd trust him with my life."

Outside, some of the storm's bite had lessened. The first pinks and oranges of the day appeared through the falling snow.

No matter what the future held, she would always remember the special time shared with Aaron. She'd hold it in her heart forever, because he made her believe she had a chance at goodness again. Whether as Amish or some other form of a simple life, it didn't matter.

"We should go, though I really hate to. This is wonderful."

He grinned. "It is. But I don't feel safe staying here too long. Those men are determined. I'll put out the fire and then we can go." Aaron went outside and scooped up some of the piled snow, then carried it inside to douse the blaze.

Once it was out, they returned to the cold. Leaving the protection of the cabin was hard. With the new day dawning, they'd be exposed each step of the way. Victoria couldn't help but believe with so many men searching for them, regardless of where they went, it was only a matter of time before she and Aaron were forced into a showdown. And she wasn't sure if they'd survive.

Frigid air wiped away the warmth they'd enjoyed from the fire in no time, as snow swirled all around them. Soon, he and Victoria were covered in a fresh blanket of snow. Moving through several feet of the thick, white accumulation slowed them down tremendously.

"How are you holding up?" Victoria asked when his footsteps slowed.

He wiped sweat from his forehead. "Ready to be warm again."

She smiled. "Me, too."

The trees had begun to thin in front of them. "We are almost to the ranch." He tried to sound positive. Lights from Ethan's house were visible, but a valley separated them from safety.

"That's a welcome sight." Victoria heaved out a huge sigh and laughed.

Aaron smiled despite his weary limbs.

Leaving the trees behind, he felt exposed almost immediately. His skin crawled. If the men were still up on the mountain, it was possible they'd be spotted.

After what felt like forever, they reached the valley floor. Ethan had several hundred head of cattle grazing here. He'd put out large rolls of hay to feed the animals during the cold. Bales were scattered all around the valley. A barn was off to the right. If they could make it there…

He stopped beside the first bale to catch his breath.

Victoria shielded her eyes as she searched the woods above them. "I don't see anyone, but I feel they're close."

The hairs raised on the back of his neck. "I feel the same way. Let's keep moving. We're almost to the barn."

Leaving the protection of the hay bale was hard.

"Keep us safe." The prayer left his lips as he stepped from their cover. Aaron kept his focus on the barn. Just a little bit farther.

Victoria's eyes darted around them. Like him, she seemed to expect another ambush at any moment.

"We're almost there," he said as much for himself as for her.

Keep walking...

Somewhere far off, an engine fired.

"Do you hear that?" She swung toward him.

Aaron searched out the sound. A side-by-side vehicle headed their way across the field. Though the vehicle was still some distance from them, Aaron recognized the driver easily enough.

"It's Ethan." The relief he felt at seeing his friend was wiped away by the sound of gunfire exploding behind them.

Victoria grabbed Aaron's arm and pulled him toward the back of the barn. Another round spewed bullets far too close.

He and Victoria hit the ground. Victoria crawled on her hands and knees in front of him, and he followed. She didn't stop until she reached the back of the barn.

"There's dozens of them. They could have more snipers in these woods to the side of us. We must keep going." Aaron no longer heard the side-by-side.

"Where's your friend?" Victoria asked when they reached the far back corner of the barn.

The side-by-side's engine revved again, a welcome sound. While he and Victoria slipped around to the side, Ethan charged toward them, dodging a blast of continuous shooting.

Ethan reached their location and whipped the side-by-side crossways. "Need a ride?" he said in typical Ethan fashion.

"Yes, we do." Aaron opened the door to the second-row seat. Victoria jumped inside and he followed.

"Stay out of sight," Ethan warned them. "We don't want them knowing you're in the four-wheeler."

Ethan punched the vehicle as fast as it would go and roared toward the house while the men spotted them and opened fire again. Bullets ricocheted off the side-by-side. The back tire blew. But Ethan never slowed.

He drove up close to the front porch, which was out of the gunmen's line of sight.

"Get inside the house. Quickly." Ethan climbed

out and opened the door for them. Aaron and Victoria piled from the side-by-side and raced inside the house.

Ethan quickly locked the door before he turned to them. "What was that all about?"

"Those men shooting at us are dirty CIA agents," Victoria said. "They're after me because they think I have something that can prove they're responsible for taking several agents' lives. Aaron's helping me. I'd be dead without him." Victoria smiled at Aaron. "We need a place to hide until those men leave. Will you help us?"

Ethan didn't hesitate. "Of course, anything I can do. I was out checking on some of the cattle when I spotted you and Aaron approaching the barn." He turned to Aaron. "This guy's a good friend of mine. If he believes in you, then I do, too." He hurried over to the back of the house. "Looks like they're heading this way. If they find you both in here, it won't be good. Right now, they didn't see me pick you up and they can't say for certain I did. Come with me."

Ethan led them toward the back of the house. "I have a panic room where you should be safe. It's virtually invisible unless you know where to look."

He pulled out his phone and typed something

into it. A door opened in the hallway, and Aaron and Victoria stepped through the opening.

"They'll come in the house one way or another. If they think I'm cooperating, they might believe you two managed to get away through the woods. The room is soundproof, so they won't be able to hear you. Once the door closes, it locks. You can open it from inside, but you can't access it from out here unless you know how. As soon as they're gone, we'll talk."

Ethan squeezed Aaron's arm and stepped out into the hall.

Aaron closed the door and heard locks slide into place, then doubled over with his hands on his knees. "That was close." He was still breathing heavily. Both of them had almost died— again. He couldn't understand this way of life one bit. Just the little that he'd participated in went against everything he believed in, and it weighed heavy on his conscience.

"It was. I sure hope this works." Victoria glanced around the small space. On one wall was a computer monitor. She touched the screen and the hall outside the panic room appeared. There were several other camera views. One showed the front door. "We can watch what's happening from here."

Aaron stood beside her and watched. Half

a dozen men approached the front of Ethan's home, all heavily armed.

"They're almost to the house." He frowned at the screen. He was worried about his friend. He'd put Ethan's life in danger by coming here. What if the men shot Ethan to gain entrance to the house?

Victoria hit a button and sound filled the room. One of the men banged on the front door. Ethan appeared on another screen.

"Federal agents." Aaron recognized the man speaking right away—he'd been outside his workshop the previous morning Logan wasn't among the group of men, though. Surprising, since he was the one calling the shots on the ground. "There were two people near your barn a few minutes ago. Where are they?"

Aaron couldn't see Ethan's expression as he spoke. "I don't know what you're talking about. I didn't see anyone but you. When I came to investigate, you guys started shooting at me. You're on private property, no less. You could have killed me."

The man didn't believe Ethan. "You were right where we saw them last. There's no way you could miss them. So, I repeat, where are they?"

Aaron couldn't imagine how Ethan kept his calm. "And I'm telling you there was no one there. If you don't believe me, you can come inside and check it out for yourself. They must have escaped through the woods near the barn."

"You're agreeing to let us search your home?" The man's face reflected suspicion.

"I am. There's nothing to hide. I'm allowing you into my home, over which you have no jurisdiction." Ethan stepped aside and the men filed in.

Armed men neared the hidden door.

"Search the house," the man who'd spoken earlier ordered. "Make sure you check all the rooms."

Several men moved past the camera's view. Other parts of the house appeared on smaller screens as the men begin their search.

"You don't want to get on the wrong side of the law on this one," the same man warned Ethan. They were standing right outside the panic room. The camera showed the man's aggressive stance. "These two are dangerous. They've killed several people. But they're not getting away this time. We're taking them with us…dead or alive."

"Believe me, I know which side I'm on." Ethan stood up to the man's intimidation. "I'm a former marine, and I'll be sure to report what's happened here to the sheriff once you and your men are gone."

Aaron's fear for his friend grew. These men were capable of great harm. They would think nothing of killing Ethan to hide their crimes.

"Go ahead. The sheriff knows all about what we're doing here. If you're lying and hiding them, he'll be sure to arrest you." The threat hung in the air between the two men.

Victoria gripped Aaron's arm. She'd mentioned something along the same lines. Was it possible the sheriff and his deputies were cooperating with these men? Aaron wouldn't believe it. He knew the sheriff. He was a *gut* man.

"Really? I happen to be acquainted with the sheriff myself," Ethan told the man.

Several men appeared on the screen again near where Ethan and the man were talking.

"Well?" the person calling the shots barked.

"The place is empty."

Aaron homed in on the man's expression. That he was angry was an understatement.

He was almost right on top of Ethan. "If you're hiding them, we will find out, and it won't be good for you. The question you have to ask yourself is are their lives worth yours?"

Ethan never flinched. The tension between the two was visible on the screen.

"Let's go. Search the property outside. All of it." The man eyed Ethan a moment longer before he stepped back. He and his people headed away from the camera with Ethan following.

The front-door camera picked them up as they left the house.

"I can't believe this is happening." Aaron headed to the door, but Victoria stopped him.

"We should wait for Ethan to tell us it's safe."

He slowly nodded. "You're right. That's smart."

"How well do you know Ethan?"

Aaron held her gaze. "He's honest, Victoria. He would not betray me."

"But he doesn't know me."

He placed his hands on her shoulders. "You can trust him, I promise."

She blew out a breath. "I'm sorry. Trust is something that's hard to come by these days."

As they continued to watch the outside cameras, the men disappeared from view. Aaron believed they would fall back and watch the house from a distance.

Minutes passed, then the door unlocked and Ethan came in. "You heard the conversation?" He glanced between them.

"We did," Aaron confirmed. "Have they left?"

"Yes, they've left the property. For now." Ethan looked past him to Victoria. "But they could be watching from a distance."

She nodded. "They probably are. I'm sorry you're in the middle of this now."

Ethan held up his hand. "I don't have to hear your side of the story to know they were lying. Typically, federal agents don't come onto private property and start shooting. And they didn't even offer their badges." He looked at Aaron. "You both have been through the ringer. Come with me and I'll get you a change of clothing and something warm to eat."

Aaron was only too happy to leave the confines of the panic room and be free of his grimy clothes.

They passed by the living room that Ethan had gone all out decorating for the holiday. An enormous tree was placed in front of some floor-to-ceiling windows. Twinkling lights covered the tree and the fireplace mantel. More lights hung from the full round log beams above.

Aaron remembered Ethan telling him how much he loved decorating for Christmas, though it had been hard since his wife's death. She'd always gone overboard with the decorating. Ethan said he never thought he'd miss having to string up so many lights until she died.

"My wife was close to your size," Ethan told Victoria and led the way to the master bedroom. "I still have her clothes in her closet. Five years and I can't seem to get rid of them. Maybe God had a reason for it. There's a bathroom through there if you want to take a shower. Her closet's that one." He pointed it out. "I'll grab Aaron something to change into and then we'll leave."

Ethan disappeared into a second closet and came out with a set of clothes. "Aaron, come with me. You can use one of the guest rooms."

They stepped out into the hall. With a searching look at Aaron, Victoria closed the door.

Aaron followed his friend to a second bedroom down the hall from the panic room.

Ethan laid the clothes on the bed. "There's the bathroom." He indicated a door. "Once you're finished, let's talk."

With those words still ringing in Aaron's ears, Ethan crossed the room and left.

Aaron held his hands out in front of him. They were still shaking from the last attack. These men were ruthless and there was no doubt in Aaron's mind that they would be plotting the next strike even now. It felt as if each second they were sitting still, they risked being captured...or worse. But if they didn't take a moment to rest, the chances of making a mistake that would get them killed were great.

He opened the door to the bathroom. A walk-in shower called out to him. The cold had penetrated straight through to his bones. His regret cut way deeper. He'd now put his friend's life at risk without having a good idea what they were running from. What did the murder of CIA agents and some illegal drugs have to do with what was happening now?

Aaron stared at the baffled man in the mirror. His face was covered in dirt, his hair matted. The injuries he'd suffered had weakened him. He wasn't sure how much more he and Victoria could take.

The scents coming from the kitchen reminded Aaron of how long it had been since he had had a decent meal.

As he neared the kitchen, he noticed Ethan stirring something on the stove. Though an unlikely pair, he and Ethan had become good friends through the years. They'd shared many earnest conversations here in this kitchen. Both were widowers. Both carried the weight of bad decisions around like a constant companion.

Ethan glanced up when he entered the room and beckoned him over. "Have a seat." He gave Aaron a cup of coffee, then returned to the stove to stir the pot once more. "Soup's almost hot. This is Jolie's potato-soup recipe. I sure hope I did it justice." Ethan turned off the burner and grabbed one of the bowls near the stove. After ladling soup, he handed the bowl to Aaron.

Bowing his head, Aaron silently poured his

heart out to *Gott*. He had no idea where to go from here and it had been hours since he'd spoken to his family. Were they safe?

He whispered "amen" in his head and opened his eyes. Ethan watched him through the steam from his coffee. Aaron couldn't imagine the questions going through Ethan's head.

"Your friend is in a lot of trouble. And I'm guessing she's not Amish despite the way she's dressed."

Aaron wanted to share what he knew, but this wasn't his story to tell. "She is not. Victoria is a former CIA agent." All of Ethan's doubts were clear as he continued to level a look at Aaron. "I should not have come here. If there were any other choice—"

"Nonsense. You are my friend and I would do anything for you, but I want to make sure you realize how much trouble you could be getting involved in."

"We've done nothing wrong. These men are the ones who should be in trouble."

"I gathered as much. Still, they obviously have a reason for coming after her so aggressively. They won't give up until someone is dead." Those words hit hard. For someone who had military training like Ethan to be worried only confirmed how bad their position was.

Ethan glanced at something behind Aaron and

he turned. Victoria stood in the doorway wearing jeans and a green sweater. Her hair—damp from the shower—hung around her shoulders.

"Come, have some soup. It will warm you up," he said, but she didn't budge. He read all the doubts on her face. She hadn't survived by trusting strangers.

"It's *oke*. Ethan is on our side."

After another second's hesitation, she let go of a breath and moved to the kitchen counter. Ethan scooped out soup and set it down in front of Victoria before sticking out his hand.

"I didn't have the chance to introduce myself properly. Ethan Connors."

She clasped his hand. "Victoria Kauffman."

"Nice to meet you, Victoria. Aaron told me some things about what's happened, but I'm guessing there's plenty more. Why don't you take a seat? Have some soup and tell me what's really going on."

THIRTEEN

Victoria pulled out the stool beside Aaron. How did she start to explain the nightmare she'd lived through for over a year?

"It's a long story, but first, I want to thank you for your help. We'd be dead if you hadn't rescued us when you did." She was stalling, gauging the man standing in front of her. The habit was hard to break when her life depended on getting it right the first time. Did she dare tell Ethan her secrets? There were few people she trusted anymore. Funny how it came easy with Aaron.

"You're welcome. I know Aaron quite well, and I consider him a friend." Ethan paused and kept his attention on her face. "I realize under the circumstances it's hard to confide in anyone, but I promise you can. So why don't you tell me why those men want you dead."

She'd been running for so long. Exhaustion had become embedded in her bones. Her thoughts were foggy and difficult to pull together from lack of sleep. She'd survived by trusting few people, and she was terrified of making the wrong decision now.

But if Aaron vouched for this man, she would trust him.

She gathered a breath. "It began a year ago in Afghanistan." She told him about the bombing and losing David and the rest of the team. The frightening events after she'd returned stateside. Discovering the evidence. Her growing suspicions about the men tracking her.

When she'd finished, Ethan blew out a long whistle. "That's an incredible story." He mulled over what she'd said. "And you've searched through all your stuff? You're positive there is no tracking device?"

"Yes, I am. Believe me, I've gone through every possible scenario. Then I realized the CIA has the capability of cloning phones. It's a quick process. They'd just need to be close enough to the target phone and have the right equipment. I ran a program to check for this. That's not how they found me—which leaves only one explanation. These men would expect I'd be in touch with my former commander at some point. They probably tapped his line to get my phone number. Then they waited for me to the turn the phone on again. As soon as it went live, they traced it. That's what I would have done." She shrugged. "At this point, they have so many men in the area, it wouldn't surprise me if they started searching every single house around."

"Unbelievable." Ethan shook his head. "Have you reached out to your commander?"

"Not since they showed up at my cabin this morning. But he needs to know he could be in trouble. Since I had to destroy my phone, would it be possible to use yours? In the past, Robert kept a burner phone that he told me only David and I had the number to. I know it's a longshot, and there's no guarantee he even still uses it, but it's worth a try. Right now, I don't see any other option."

"Of course." Ethan pulled out his phone and handed it to her.

Victoria dialed the number only to have it go to voice mail. She shook her head. "He's not picking up." She handed the phone back to Ethan. Was Robert okay?

The longer they remained at Ethan's home, the more likely it was that the men would return. "I'm putting you in danger by being here, Ethan. I should leave." She looked to Aaron. "And I have no doubt those men will come back. You and Ethan should both find someplace safe to stay for a while—"

He didn't let her finish. "We've been through

this. I'm not letting you face those men by yourself."

"Aaron's right," Ethan said. "You can't do this alone." He indicated her bowl of soup getting cold. "Finish your meal, both of you. I'm going to have a look outside to see if there's any sign of those thugs. When I come back, let's have a look at that evidence. Maybe with a fresh set of eyes we'll find something useful."

That promise rang in her ears as Ethan left the room.

The weight of the past year, filled with doubts and misdirection, lifted. Now, for the first time since David uttered those disturbing words, she believed it might be possible to figure out the truth.

Facing Aaron, she slowly smiled. He'd given her back the possibility of a future. It was in her grasp and she couldn't wait. "You should see if Ethan has someone who can check on your family." She couldn't imagine how worried Aaron must be for them.

"Ethan has lots of friends in this valley," he murmured without looking away.

Her smile disappeared. Her feelings for Aaron grew stronger with each look, each smile. And she believed he cared about her, as well. She'd give anything to be able to take his hand and tell him how she felt. But now was not the right time. Would there ever be one?

She thought about the past. Even when she was still with the CIA and her heart belonged to David, she'd known the spy life wasn't what she wanted for herself long-term. This past year, she'd been so devastated by his death that she hadn't thought about what their future might have looked like. David was a career agent. He wouldn't have wanted to leave the excitement behind.

Aaron made her see the future she wanted. The life that had been taken from her once seemed possible, and for that she was grateful.

She touched his face, feeling the soft beard growth beneath her fingers. "I'm so glad you're with me." Even though she'd put him at risk, she couldn't imagine doing this without him.

He clasped her hand in both of his. Calluses on his palms spoke of the hard work he did for his family—the ones she'd put in danger.

Tears clogged her throat. "You didn't ask for any of this, and I'm sorry."

He clutched her hand against his chest. "I would do it again because you are worth it." He leaned his head against hers. "We'll get through this. And when we do…" He didn't finish, yet the promise left unspoken made her heart soar.

"They seem to have cleared out…" Neither

had heard Ethan return. They broke apart guiltily. Ethan stopped halfway into the kitchen and glanced between them. "Am I interrupting something?"

Victoria pulled her hand free and shook her head.

A second more passed before Ethan said, "I called my foreman, who went to buy feed, and told him not to come back here until we're sure it's safe." With another curious look, Ethan poured himself some coffee and leaned on the counter.

Not for a moment did Victoria believe the men had left the area. They wouldn't give up that easy. They were waiting somewhere to make their next move. If Ethan hadn't been home, the outcome today would have been far more deadly.

"Do you think your foreman would mind checking on my family?" Aaron explained about sending them to his friend's house.

"Not at all. I'll give Jim a call right now. Excuse me." Ethan turned away.

When it was just the two of them again, Victoria rose a little unsteadily. "I'll go get the photos." She left without looking at Aaron and struggled to reclaim her composure.

Victoria closed the bedroom door and leaned against it. What was wrong with her? If she survived this, she and Aaron would probably never see each other again. She couldn't let herself fall in love with him.

She lifted the handmade metal box that held the photos. Though she still had no idea how David had gotten the photos in the storage facility, she was certain he had help.

Victoria had packed David's clothing away in a box. She hadn't been able to look at them for a long time. Then, two weeks ago, she'd finally opened the box and found the key hidden in the lining of David's old boots. She'd destroyed the boots and the rest of his clothing. The only things she'd kept were his grandfather's lighter, his Glock and David's old busted-up cell because the screen saver was a picture of them together at a happier time. With the battery damaged beyond salvaging, the phone hadn't worked. She'd made sure there was no tracking device inside it. At some point, when she had her life back, she wanted to retrieve the photo even if she had to go to David's service carrier and ask for their help.

She slipped the phone in her pocket, carried the box to the kitchen and set it on the counter.

Ethan's attention fixed on the box. "That's unusual." He picked it up to examine. "It's made of thick metal. Whoever created it wanted to make sure it could withstand a fire. Did it belong to your friend?" He placed the box back on the counter.

"I'd never seen it before I found it in the storage unit, but I'm guessing it did." She removed the surveillance photos and spread them across the counter. "This is what David left me. There are five surveillance photos in all. I believe they were all taken in Afghanistan, but at different times. One at night." She pointed to that one. "The rest were taken during the day. Several show a truck moving something through the country. These two are from some type of desert meeting in a rudimentary camp. Only one person is clear enough to identify. The rest, not so much."

She dug into the box and brought out the photo of the ledger. "This I don't understand at all. It's a photo of a ledger containing nothing but groups of numbers." Victoria shook her head. She'd gone through them dozens of times, but still had no clearer idea of what they meant than the first time she'd looked at them.

Ethan picked up one of the photos of the truck. He rummaged through a kitchen drawer until he found a magnifying glass and held it near the photo. "There's definitely something stashed back there. I can't make it out, though." He directed his attention to the terrain around the truck and shook his head. "It could be anywhere in Afghanistan." He picked up a second photo taken at night. It showed what appeared to be the same truck, without its lights on, moving down a rudimentary road. Whatever it was carrying, the driver was doing his best to keep it a secret.

Ethan was a veteran, and had seen combat. She'd hoped he would pick up on something she hadn't.

"You're right, it could be." Victoria tried to keep her disappointment to herself as she told him where they were at the time of the bombing. "These were obviously taken some time before that. David had the chance to print them out and store them."

Ethan picked up the photo of the ledger. "I don't get this one. Maybe the numbers are some type of longitude and latitude coordinates?"

"I thought of that, but the numbers aren't long enough." David had gone to such lengths to hide the photos, and she was positive he'd done his best to make sure she was the one who found the storage key. If only he'd been more specific about what he was trying to tell her.

Aaron picked up one of the photos and stared at it. "I know this man."

Victoria whipped toward him, his revelation coming as a surprise. "You do? How?"

Aaron pointed to the one man who appeared

to be staring right at the camera. "That's Mike Logan." She hadn't gotten a good look at the man who had identified himself as Logan, but Aaron had.

The grainy image showed a man covered from head to toe in dark clothing, as if deliberately trying to disguise his appearance. He wore a knit cap that concealed his hair.

She took the photo from him. All she could see was his face. Was there something vaguely familiar about it, or was she simply grasping for straws?

Aaron had no doubt the man was Mike Logan. "Do you know him?" he asked when he noticed the way she frowned at the photo.

She focused on Logan for a long time before shaking her head. "I'm not sure."

"There has to be more than what we're seeing here." Ethan paused to think for a moment. "Look, I know you don't trust going to the sheriff right now, and with good reason, but since we can't reach your former commander yet, do you mind if I take a picture of the ledger and send it to a military friend of mine? He's a genius at decoding. I won't mention you, but I'm all out of ideas and I'm afraid we'll never figure out what David was trying to tell us on our own."

"You think it's some type of code?" Victoria's doubts were clear in her voice.

"It's possible," Ethan said and stared at the numbers.

Victoria glanced out the kitchen window. "I think we should get out of here while we still can. Have no doubt, those men will come back."

"I agree with you," Ethan said with a nod. "Grab your stuff and come with me."

Victoria tossed the photos into the box, along with David's old phone, and closed the lid.

Ethan led them to an attached garage, where a large SUV was parked. "They're on foot and this thing is pretty much bulletproof."

Ethan hopped behind the wheel. Aaron climbed in next to him while Victoria slid in back.

"This SUV has four-wheel drive, so we should be able to go cross-country in case they're watching the roads." Ethan opened the garage and reversed. Once they cleared the building, he shoved the SUV into Drive and drove out past the back of the house while Aaron grabbed hold of the armrest and hung on as they began to traverse the rocky countryside.

"I see movement in the woods to your right," Victoria warned. The words barely cleared her lips when a half dozen men emerged from the woods and opened fire. Ethan swerved to avoid a hit. The vehicle plowed through thick snow.

Aaron peered through the side window as their attackers continued to shoot at them. "They were probably watching the place from these woods."

"Hang on. I'm going to try to get away before they shoot out a tire." Ethan floored the pedal and the SUV slipped and slid across the rough ground while bullets continued to strike all around. "It's not safe to go to your friend's house. We don't want these people following us there." Ethan kept his full attention on the path ahead. "Is there someone else you trust?"

Aaron struggled to come up with an answer. Anyone he chose would be in danger. There was only one person he could think of who might be secluded enough to escape notice.

"My cousin Harrison. His place is pretty isolated, and he's from my *mamm's* side of the family. They might not tie him to me." Aaron gave directions to his cousin's home. He and Harrison had been close growing up and remained so today. He could count on Harrison to have his back.

"Looks like we've lost them for now," Victoria said and faced forward. "But they'll radio their men who are mobile to search the roads. They'll be looking for this vehicle."

Ethan glanced briefly at her. "I'll see if I can find a way out without using the normal roads." He jerked the wheel hard and steered the vehicle around a downed tree. The going was rough due to the number of trees that had succumbed to a recent beetle infestation. It took all of Ethan's skills to keep them out of trouble.

"There's a forest-service road a little way from here, as I recall," Ethan said. "We'll use it."

Aaron struggled to make sense of the things they knew so far. At some point, Logan had been part of whatever was going on in Afghanistan. Was it all because of drugs? It seemed a great length to go just to keep a smuggling ring secret.

Ethan's phone rang. He answered it and listened. "Thanks, Jim, that's good news." He ended the call and dropped the phone on the console between them. "Jim arrived at your friend's place. Your family is safe. So far, there hasn't been anyone snooping around the farm."

All Aaron could think about was Caleb. If anything happened to his precious *sohn*…

Victoria squeezed his shoulder. "He'll be okay," she said, as if reading his thoughts. "He has his uncles looking out for him."

He forced a smile and tried his best to believe her, but it was hard. He'd thought the same about

Irene and she hadn't been okay. She'd died. He couldn't lose his *sohn*, too.

"There's the forest-service road." Ethan whipped onto it and kept going as fast as the road allowed.

Things were quickly spinning out of their control. Other innocent lives were at stake now. And they were no closer to having the answers necessary to end this nightmare than when he'd first found Victoria hiding in his workshop.

FOURTEEN

Why did Mike Logan appear so familiar? She didn't recognize the name. Victoria thought about that final trip abroad. As she recalled, Trevor had gathered little information from his asset at that point, but the promise was big. Heroin was being bartered for weapons. Massive amounts of weapons, according to Trevor, were falling into the hands of terrorists.

The asset had picked the location because he was nervous—terrified—of being found out by someone with a whole lot of power.

She recalled the brief conversation she and David had before they'd left for their destination. He'd been on edge, but she hadn't really thought much of it at the time. Everyone on the mission was anxious.

Looking back with the advantage of hindsight, she now understood that something else was troubling David. She wished she'd taken the time to ask. Wished he'd shared his suspicions.

"We're approaching your cousin's place." Ethan nodded toward the small drive coming up in front of them. "Do you think he'll mind if we get the SUV into the barn and out of sight?"

Aaron shook his head. "He won't. I sure hope we aren't bringing our troubles to Harrison and his family. His Ruth is expecting their first child soon."

Victoria fought back guilt. More innocent lives were being dragged into the line of fire because of her.

"There's Harrison," Aaron said. An Amish man around Aaron's age stepped out onto the porch and watched their approach. "Give me a moment to explain what's happening, and then I'm sure we can use the barn to put away the SUV."

The SUV rolled to a stop in front of the house and Aaron jumped out. From the back seat, Victoria watched him approach his cousin. The surprise on the man's face was soon replaced with happiness at seeing his cousin.

"They'll keep coming." Ethan turned in his seat to face her. "These men are dangerous because they hide behind the backing of the CIA, though I doubt the Agency knows anything about what they're really doing."

His words reaffirmed everything she believed. "If it's okay with you, I'd like to try reaching out to Robert again. We really need his help before someone innocent ends up dead."

Ethan handed her the phone. She dialed the number, but the call wouldn't connect. A glance at the service indicator confirmed her suspicions—not even a single bar. "There's no service." She handed him back the phone.

"It can be sketchy in many places around the community. You can walk ten feet in a different direction and sometimes pick up a signal. Once we get inside, there might be some service. There's a little bit more elevation."

Her thoughts swam. Until she could reach Robert, they were on their own. Figuring out the significance of the ledger was crucial.

Aaron came back to the SUV. "Harrison's going to open the barn for you." He climbed in and indicated Ethan should follow his cousin. "He said he hasn't seen anyone around the farm, but their place is isolated and at the edge of the community. No one comes here without a purpose."

"That's good to hear." Ethan smiled briefly. He put the SUV into gear and drove toward the barn.

After dodging the cow stabled inside because of the weather, Ethan parked the vehicle. They all climbed out and went outside to where Harrison waited.

The tall, slender-built Amish man held onto

his hat against the blustery wind. The only resemblance to Aaron was the color of his hair and beard.

"Come inside the house where it's warm," Harrison said once the introductions were made, then he faced his cousin. "Ruth will be happy to see you. She was pleased with the preserves your *mamm* brought for her to the Sunday service. *Gut* with a hot biscuit on a cold day."

Aaron smiled as they all fell into step beside his cousin.

"These men who are chasing you—do you know what they want?" Harrison's gaze shifted to Victoria.

She debated on how much to say. The less this man and his wife knew about what was happening, the better, but he deserved an explanation.

"To be honest, I'm not sure yet. They think I know something that threatens their freedom." Victoria blew out a breath that fogged the air in front of her. The cold wasn't letting up. "But I have no idea what that is." If all she had to go on for answers were the surveillance photos and the ledger that didn't make sense, she was in real trouble.

Harrison accepted her answer without questioning it. He trusted his cousin and, therefore, her.

He opened the door and stepped inside, then waited for them to do the same.

A petite woman stepped from the kitchen. Her dark blue dress, covered with an apron, revealed she was very much pregnant. Light brown hair peeked out from under her prayer *kapp*. She froze at the sight of so many people in her tiny living room. Her troubled brown eyes scanned each face before finding her husband's.

Harrison went to his wife's side. "Aaron has asked for our help." He explained the few details Aaron gave him. Nothing about what he said eased the crease from Ruth's forehead, but she welcomed them.

"I told them you were preparing the meal. Looks like we will have guests." Harrison clasped his wife's hand and faced them. "Please, warm yourselves by the fire. I will assist Ruth with the food."

The couple disappeared into the kitchen, where their quiet conversation drifted into the living room.

Victoria sank down onto the sofa and held her hands near the fire. Its warmth chased some of the chill from her body.

"I feel as if I should be doing something," she told Aaron when he took the seat beside her. "Searching for answers. Making a plan. Something."

He turned his face toward her and smiled.

"For now, rest. Then we will work out a plan. Together."

She liked the way he said "together" a little too much. This past year she'd been so lonely, fighting a battle she didn't understand. Her only contact with the world she left behind was snatches of conversation with Robert. The isolation had been crippling at times. This Christmas, being back among the Amish...well, she'd hoped for a different outcome. Maybe with a Christmas filled with peace and joy, the dangerous past she'd survived would grow more distant with each passing day.

Victoria covered his hand with hers briefly. "I'm going to take a look out the window first. Just to be safe." Though her body craved sleep, she couldn't wind down. Too many things hung in the balance. Lives were at stake. She'd witnessed enough death to last her a lifetime. She wasn't about to let anyone else die so that a group of criminals could stay out of prison.

"I spoke to Jim again," Ethan said, and stuck his phone back into his pocket. "So far everything is quiet there. Your family is worried about you, but otherwise fine. They're safe."

Aaron was grateful to his friend for checking on his loved ones. "*Denki,* Ethan. For everything."

"You're welcome." Ethan pulled up a chair next to Aaron, his attention on Victoria. "She has a lot of problems following her around."

Aaron turned and studied his friend's profile. "She does."

Ethan faced him with his eyebrows raised slightly. "You sure there's not more happening between you two than a need to help?"

He was ready to deny it, but his heart wouldn't let him.

"I see the way you look at her," Ethan continued. "I know how hard it's been for you losing Irene, but even if Victoria gets out of this thing alive, you two are from different worlds, and she has scars you know nothing about."

Ethan had his best interests at heart, but still, hearing the truth aloud was hard to take.

"There's nothing going on between us but friendship." Yet even to his own ears the answer rang false.

"All right." Ethan stood. "I'm going to grab another cup of coffee. Can I bring you one?"

Aaron shook his head and waited until Ethan stepped away. Unable to stop himself, he rose and went over to Victoria. Her shoulder muscles were taut. She wouldn't be able to relax until this thing ended. No matter what the future held, he wouldn't regret one moment of the time he'd spent with her.

She turned when he got close.

"Do you see something out there?" He searched the outdoors beyond the window. The drive they'd traveled down cut through a small yard buried in snow. Beyond, rows and rows of lodgepole pines provided coverage, yet prevented them from seeing what might be lurking on the other side.

"No, and I'm worried. I'm going to see if I can use Ethan's phone again and find a spot with enough service to call Robert. What's happening here is so far beyond my scope of understanding, it's not even funny. And I'm sorry that you and your family and friends are caught up in my problems. But I am grateful for everything you've done." She smiled into his eyes. "I've been running for my life since David died, and I'm still no closer to understanding what is happening than when he passed. Living in the shadows, unable to make a connection with anyone except Robert—and even that only from a distance—has been hard. You've made me feel as if it isn't just me against the world. I haven't felt that way in a long time."

As he looked at this strong woman, he realized because of her he didn't feel so lonely anymore, either. He brushed back the hair from her face. She stirred his heart, made him see it was possible to move beyond the cloud of grief he'd existed in for so long. Victoria gave him hope.

"Aaron…" She said his name so softly, and yet it sounded beautiful. The world around them stopped existing for a moment. It was just the two of them and he wanted to say things that he couldn't because it wasn't his right.

Letting her go was the hardest thing, but if he continued to hope for the impossible, his heart would never heal.

He stepped back. "I'll send Ethan over with the phone. I believe he made a call to his foreman so you should have service. In the meantime, Harrison and I will check around the property to be sure those men haven't found us." Without looking at her, he headed back over to Ethan. "She wants to use the phone to try and reach her former commander."

If Ethan detected anything off in Aaron's behavior, he kept it to himself. "Of course. I'll take it over now. The sooner she reaches this man, the better it will be for all of us."

Aaron watched as Ethan went over to where Victoria stared out the window. She turned as he approached, a sad smile on her face. She and Ethan exchanged a few words before he handed the phone to her. And Aaron couldn't take his eyes off her. What would she be like without this threat hanging over her head?

More than anything he wanted to be there when that moment happened.

Beside him, Harrison cleared his throat and Aaron swung to face his cousin's probing gaze. He hadn't realized Harrison was nearby. Aaron could feel the heat creeping up his neck.

"You look at her differently," Harrison said quietly.

Aaron forced himself to face his cousin. What Harrison said came close to what Ethan had mentioned earlier. Was he being so obvious that those closest to him noticed his reaction to Victoria?

"You have feelings for this woman." It wasn't a question. Aaron drew in a breath. Tried to deny it. Couldn't. Harrison voiced the same concerns as Ethan. The ones Aaron had for himself. "She is in a lot of trouble, and she is an *Englischer.*"

"I know all these things, cousin, and I don't plan on acting on my feelings. My life is here, in West Kootenai. It's all I know."

"You've been lonely since Irene's passing. Perhaps it is time to consider remarrying another woman from the community. For Caleb's sake…and for yours."

The idea of sharing his life with another was not something he'd considered before Victoria.

Her eyes locked with his across the room and a hint of a smile crossed her face as she put the phone to her ear and listened. He couldn't look away. Something about her pulled him in, made him have hope.

Ethan came over to where he and his cousin were, and Aaron was happy for the interruption.

"We should check around the property to make sure those men aren't close," Aaron told them both, yet he didn't move.

Victoria turned toward the window once more. From her worried expression he had a feeling she hadn't been able to reach her commander.

"That's a good idea," Ethan said and started for the door. Aaron and Harrison followed him outside.

Before they could start their perimeter check, the door opened, and Victoria stepped onto the porch.

"Robert's not answering the burner," she told them. "I'll keep trying. I sure hope he has the phone still and thinks to check it." She shook her head. "I want to help with the search. This is my problem and I'm not letting you all risk your lives while I wait inside." She squared her shoulders with a determined look on her face that discouraged an argument.

"We'll cover more ground with added people. Harrison, why don't you come with me?" Ethan said. "Victoria, you and Aaron take the front of the property. We'll go around back. If you hear anything, come get us. We'll do the same." Ethan looked from one to the other before he and Harrison headed around the side of the house and out of sight.

As Aaron walked beside Victoria, all he could think about was the uncomfortable conversations with Harrison and Ethan.

"You must be worried about your family," she said as they neared the woods that lined the drive.

He glanced her way. "Ethan spoke to them again. Everyone is safe." Ignoring the warnings of his heart, he reached for her hand. She slowly stopped and turned to him.

"This isn't your fault. Not what happened to David and your other team members. And not what's happening now."

Her pretty mouth twisted into a bitter smile. "Isn't it? I should have known something was going on with David. I did know. Why didn't I ask more questions? If I had, he might still be alive."

He tugged her closer and tipped her chin back so he could look into her eyes. "Or you might be dead, as well. Someone figured out David was on to them and they had to eliminate him. They didn't care who else they took out in the process. And they don't care now."

She leaned against him and his pulse responded with a fierce beat. He gathered her closer and held her because it felt right.

"When this is over, I don't ever want to be part of another undercover operation again," she whispered against his chest. "I want out. I want a better way of life. A simpler one."

Aaron froze upon hearing those words. He couldn't let himself have hope. She was tired and upset and wasn't thinking clearly. Living the Plain life was not easy, and she'd been away from it for too long.

He let her go and struggled for something to say.

When she started walking again, he fell into step, glad she didn't seem to expect a response.

The woods, filled with untouched snow, unfolded before them. Victoria scanned the ground in front of them. "There's no sign anyone's been here recently. Let's head out to the road before we go back to the others."

Staying in the woods, they were almost to the road when Victoria suddenly stopped. She was listening for something. A moment later, he heard it. A vehicle.

Aaron eased closer to the road. A car rolled down it at a slow pace. He recognized the vehicle from before. It was the same car that had followed them. Somehow, they'd been found again.

FIFTEEN

"We have to warn the others," she whispered. Adrenaline pumped through her limbs as the car turned onto the gravel path. It was heading for Harrison's house.

Ethan and Harrison waited at the clearing between the house and woods. They'd heard the noise.

"Get out of sight before they get here." Victoria waved them toward the house. She and Aaron raced inside behind them.

When Victoria crossed the threshold, she shut the door and slid the lock into place. At the window, she parted the curtains enough to see out. The car slowly eased toward the house.

"They'll recognize Ethan, Aaron and me for sure. Is there someplace where we can hide?"

"Our bedroom." Harrison dashed down the hall and opened the door. "Quickly."

Victoria stepped into the room, along with Aaron and Ethan.

"If they ask to search the place, you have the right to refuse," Victoria told Harrison. "Use the excuse your wife isn't feeling well. Something. Just don't let them inside."

"I will try," Harrison said, but his eyes were wide and fearful as he closed the door.

"There's a good chance this will go south quickly." Ethan looked her in the eye as he said those chilling words. "It could get dangerous real fast."

She knew what he meant. They could be forced into a shoot-out with these men. If so, they'd be putting Harrison and Ruth in the middle.

Outside, car doors slammed while Victoria tried to determine how many. Three, she believed.

She leaned against the door and listened. Footsteps moved along the porch. Someone banged against the door. The noise set her nerves on edge.

Harrison's quiet voice could be heard speaking.

"We're looking for this woman. We have reason to believe she's here. Have you seen her?" She recognized the man's voice right away. Logan. The man in the photo. Possibly the same person who had killed David and the rest of her team.

Anger burned deep down in her heart. The

desire to rush out and confront him with what she knew was strong. She wanted to hurt him the way he had so many others. But if she did, she'd end up getting innocent people killed.

"There's no one here but me and my wife, and she is pregnant," Harrison said.

Silence followed. Victoria held her breath. Would Logan buy the excuse and leave, or storm the house?

Please, Lord...no.

"We're coming inside." Sounds of shoving were followed by the slamming of the door against the wall.

"Over by the door," Victoria said. "When they come inside, we'll be hidden by it. Be ready. They'll be here soon."

Her heartbeat was so loud she couldn't hear anything else as they huddled together. The door flew open and three men charged into the room.

Right now, they had the element of surprise. It wouldn't last. Victoria nodded to Ethan and they charged from their hiding place.

All three men closed in. Victoria struck one with the butt of her weapon and he went down hard.

"Aaron, watch out!" she yelled as a second man grabbed him by his shoulder. Victoria ran to help. Logan cut her off. She was inches from the business end of a semiautomatic rifle.

"You should have stayed out of it." His finger was on the trigger. She had seconds to live and only one choice. She dove for Logan, hitting the arm holding the weapon. It fired. The bullets missed her by inches as they slammed into the opposing wall.

Logan stumbled backward with her holding on. She fought with all her strength to get the weapon out of his hand, but Logan was stronger. Victoria grabbed the barrel of the weapon and didn't let go.

With a snarl, Logan slugged her hard enough to send her flying across the room. The world blurred. She shook her head to clear her vision. Before she could right herself, he aimed the gun at her head. Victoria closed her eyes. A shot from a handgun rang out.

Aaron struggled to free himself from his captor before the man shot him. He had the weapon in position, but his focus suddenly shifted to something beyond Aaron's shoulder. Before Aaron could turn, another shot rang out. The man dropped to the ground with a bullet through his chest.

Aaron jerked toward the person who'd fired. Ethan had saved his life.

All he could think about was Victoria. He'd heard another shot earlier. As he neared the place where she was, he noticed Logan had landed on top of her.

With Ethan's help, they pulled the dead man off her and she moaned and tried to sit up.

Aaron dropped to his knees. "Are you hurt?"

She shook her head and winced. "I'm okay." But she had to say it twice before he was convinced.

Logan had a single gunshot wound to the back of his head. Ethan's aim had been lethal.

The last man was lying in an unconscious heap near where Ethan had taken him down.

"Let's get the third man tied up before he wakes." Victoria indicated the unconscious man. She searched around the room for something to use as a restraint and found nothing.

Harrison and Ruth appeared in the doorway.

Ruth's hand flew to cover her mouth when she spotted the dead men lying in their bedroom. Harrison gathered her close and tucked her head against his shoulder to shield her from the disturbing scene.

"Do you have rope or something we can use as a restraint?" Victoria asked.

Ruth managed a nod without looking her way. "I will go get it." She stumbled from the room.

Victoria searched Logan's pockets and located his cell phone. She scanned through the phone numbers. "I don't recognize any of his contacts."

Ruth returned with the rope but didn't enter the room. She kept her gaze averted. Victoria took the rope and she and Aaron secured the unconscious man.

"Ethan, if I have your permission, I'd like to take some photos of Logan and these two men. Maybe Robert will recognize them."

"Good thinking. Do it."

She clicked photos. With a final look at Logan, she escorted Ruth and Harrison outside to the barn. It was no longer safe for them to remain in their own home.

Aaron quickly unbolted the door while Ethan pulled out the SUV. As soon as they were all inside, Ethan headed out behind the house. "It's too risky to use the road," he told them. "We're sure to run in to more of Logan's men. By now, they have the whole community teeming with people searching for us."

Aaron leaned back against the seat. "If Logan is dead, then perhaps this—whatever this is— ends with him." He glanced back at Victoria, who shook her head.

"I wish I could believe that, but these men have gone to great lengths to get the evidence David left behind and silence me. I need to know why." She stopped for a second. "And I don't think Logan is the actual man in charge. There's someone else above him, someone with a lot of power. We really could use Robert's help."

She dialed the phone again. "Hello? Robert?" Surprise showed on her face as she sat up straighter. "It's me. Something's happened." Victoria gave the details as quickly as possible. When she'd finished, she listened. Soon, a look of relief spread across her face. "Thank you, Robert. Thank you so much." She ended the call.

"He's assembling a team to extract us. Until we can figure out what's really going on here, it's not safe for you or your family to remain here," she told Aaron. "You'll need to come with us. You should as well, Ethan. I pray we'll have answers soon and you all can return to your lives. As soon as he has news of where we can meet, he'll call. This is almost over." Her eyes shone with happiness. "We just have to stay out of sight for a little while longer."

With his life in turmoil, one word hung in Aaron's head like an unwelcome thought. Over. These past few days had changed his life—not just because of the bad things that had happened, but because of her. Victoria. He hadn't meant to fall for this special *Englisch* woman, and yet he had. She'd faced each deadly encounter without faltering, and all because of a commitment she'd made to someone she cared about. Soon, the trouble they faced would end. She'd be gone from his life. Did he possess the courage necessary to do the right thing and let her go? Only *Gott* knew.

SIXTEEN

This is almost over.

She sat back in her seat and closed her eyes. Almost over. Why didn't it feel like it? Because too many questions remained unanswered. It wouldn't be finished until she knew the real reason behind David and her teammates' deaths.

The SUV made an unexpected turn, and her eyes flew open. "Where are we?" Even with Robert's assurances, she couldn't relax.

"This is Jonah's home. No one knows about this place and he is not part of my family. We should be safe enough here." Aaron watched her with narrowed eyes. She couldn't imagine how messed up she must look right now. She was scared out of her mind, jumping at sounds.

The gnawing in her gut wouldn't allow her to believe they could be safe.

Snowy trees passed by the window, reminding her that it was now Christmas Eve. Tomorrow was Christmas. Would she be spending the holiday on the run or moving toward the future she longed for—a simple one here in West Kootenai? Her attention was drawn to Aaron. When this ended would they say goodbye? The thought hurt so much. She cared for him deeply. She hadn't meant to give away her heart, but Aaron was so easy to love.

"There's Jonah." She looked to where Aaron indicated. A man stood in front of a white clapboard house, which was like so many of the others in this Amish country.

Ethan pulled the vehicle up next to him. Bright red hair poked out from beneath his hat. His matching beard was dotted with snowflakes.

Aaron lowered his window and clasped Jonah's hand, a smile on his handsome face for his friend. "It is *gut* to see you."

"You, too, my friend." Jonah looked back at the house, where the door had opened, and Caleb was now racing toward the vehicle.

"Daed!"

Jonah stepped aside. Aaron hopped out and scooped his son into his arms, hugging him tight. The love between the two reminded her of the danger she'd brought to their innocent door. All because of what had happened on the other side of the world in Afghanistan. All because of secrets someone wanted to stay buried.

"I was so afraid." The young boy wept as he gulped out the words and scrubbed a fist across his face.

"I'm *oke*," Aaron said, soothing his son's tears. "I'm *oke*." Over the top of the boy's head, his eyes met Victoria's. Compassion burned deep. Would he blame her in time? She certainly did.

Aaron returned to the SUV, and Caleb hopped onto his lap. The boy didn't want to let his father out of his sight again.

"You can pull into the barn. Your foreman parked his truck there, but both vehicles should fit."

Ethan nodded. "Jim's a good friend. We can use his help."

"For sure," Jonah said with a nod. "Follow me to the barn." Jonah headed to open the door for them.

Ethan crept the SUV along until it fitted into the tight space. With only a few inches to spare, he parked and killed the engine.

They squeezed out of the vehicle and went inside.

Her eyes wide and fearful, Aaron's mother rushed to her son as soon as he entered. "I've been so worried." She hugged him close.

"I know, but we are all fine. A little weary, but otherwise, *oke*." Aaron smiled over at Harrison and Ruth before explaining the news from Victoria's commander.

Martha clasped her hands together. "This is *gut* to hear. We need help. There are so many of them."

Aaron kept his arm around his *mamm* as he moved closer to the fire. Watching the two together reminded Victoria of the woman who had meant the world to her, and she looked away.

She still clutched Ethan's phone in her hand. Robert had reiterated only she and David knew about his burner phone. There would be no way for these men to track it. She quickly sent the photos she'd taken to Robert, almost certain he'd recognize Logan from some of his surveillances.

There was nothing left to do but wait, yet Victoria couldn't settle down. She opened the box again and spread the photos out on the kitchen table, searching for something to tie what little they knew together. With the phone gripped tightly in her hand, she checked for messages periodically. Her tormented thoughts were unable to shut down. Would Robert's men arrive too late to save them?

"How are you holding up?" She jumped at the sound of Aaron's voice so close. She hadn't realized he was near until he spoke.

"Worried. Unable to relax. I'm ready for this

to end." She forced a smile while searching his face. Would he be happy to have his life return to normal when that happened? Would her heart ever recover from the loss of losing him? As she stared at his handsome face, so many questions came to mind. She didn't ask any of them because she had no right.

His eyes softened as he skimmed her face, and her chest tightened at the tenderness there. It would be so easy to let go, to love him completely. But she couldn't. Aaron deserved so much more than the broken-down killer who stood before him now.

Victoria's attention fell on David's phone, then on the one in her hand. They were identical. Somehow, David had gotten the photos to the storage facility. What if there was something else on the phone that might help her understand what was happening? What if the answers she needed were right there with her all along and she'd been too concerned with staying alive to realize it?

She swung toward Ethan. "Do you mind if I try something with your phone's battery?"

Ethan came over to where she stood. "What do you have in mind?"

Victoria indicated the phone that David had carried with him on that final mission. "This belonged to David. It was destroyed in the explosion. The battery was damaged. I don't know why I didn't think of this earlier." She shook her head. Why hadn't she? The only explanation was she'd been too busy trying to save her own life. She wouldn't have kept the phone except for the screen-saver photo. Had that been at God's urging?

"You have the same type of phone. If I can put your battery in his phone, I might be able to get it to work again." She glanced sideways to Ethan.

"It's worth a try."

Victoria removed the battery from Ethan's phone and put it into the damaged one. With the battery in place, she turned on David's phone.

"It's coming up." Aaron looked over her shoulder.

She watched in amazement as the phone powered on. When the screen saver appeared, Victoria went to work. It didn't take her long to come up with something. "Whoa. These are the same photos that were in the storage facility. He took them with this phone." She showed the photos to Aaron and Ethan. There was a date imprinted on them. She pointed to it. "That's about a month before his death."

She continued to search the phone's contents. "This is interesting. It appears David texted these photos to Wes Sorenson. That's David's high-school friend." There was no note attached to the text. She believed somehow David had reached out to Wes and had him put the photos in the storage unit.

"When did the bombing happen?" Ethan asked.

"November twentieth of last year."

"The message was sent two weeks before that. Was Wes at the funeral?" Ethan focused on her again.

"He wasn't." At the time, she'd been too broken up to think about it.

"Seems strange that a friend that close wouldn't be at the service," Ethan mused aloud. "Are there any calls between the two?"

She pulled up the call log. "Yes, there are several."

"Once you've finished searching David's phone, you should reach out to Wes and see what he remembers from those calls," Aaron said. "He might be able to explain why David sent him the photos in the first place. I'm guessing Wes was the one who put them in the storage facility for David."

Victoria nodded. "That makes sense." She stopped when she found a file that David had hidden in a location on the phone, where he must have believed it wouldn't easily be found. She opened it. The file contained a single video.

Her fingers shook as she hit Play. David's face appeared on the screen, taking her breath away.

"Victoria, I don't have much time, but I want you to know if anything happens to me, Trevor Hawk is the one behind this. Trevor has been transporting something illegal across the country. Heroin would be my guess, but I can't say for sure. I followed him when I became suspicious. Someone else is helping him. Someone from the base by the name of Mike Logan." Victoria's gaze shot to Aaron's. The person who had been leading the charge to kill them was Trevor's accomplice. Was Logan the asset they were supposed to meet before the bombing, or had that all been a lie?

"All the proof you need to bring Trevor down is on my phone and in my storage locker. I asked Wes to set it up under my alias—you know the one." A noise in the background had David jerking around. He was clearly nervous and lowered his voice. "I suspect Trevor knows I'm on to him. There's something different in the way he looks at me. He's suspicious and he's planning something, I'm sure of it. Stop him, Victoria. Don't let him get away with it. Please. For me." The recording ended abruptly.

Victoria fought back tears and pulled in a ragged breath. Seeing David again—hearing his voice—brought it all back. How tragic it was that David had given his life because of someone's greed.

"Who is this man he's speaking of? You've mentioned him before." Aaron studied her reaction.

She struggled to process everything David had said. Could he have been wrong about Trevor?

"He was the one who oversaw the last mission. It was his asset we were meeting..." She stopped as a horrifying thought occurred. "But he's dead. Trevor Hawk died in the explosion."

"Maybe Mike Logan lured Trevor to the location to take him out?" Ethan said.

She tried the theory on for size, but it didn't fit in her mind. "But why? David said Logan was stationed at the base. I'm guessing he meant Bagram Air Base. Still, Logan would need Trevor to help him transport the drugs out of the country without being detected."

"Unless maybe he didn't execute Trevor at all..." Ethan held her gaze.

"You think Trevor didn't really die." Victoria tried to piece together how it would be possible. "He was the first to go into the building. There's no way he could have survived."

"Are you sure? His body was identified?" Ethan asked, pressing for answers.

She remembered every second of that night.

The explosion took everyone by surprise. She and David, the last inside, were badly hurt. He'd tried to get her out of the sniper fire, and he had, but not without cost. Both of them were flown to Bagram Air Base. David hung on for weeks. When he awoke, she thought he was going to be okay. And then he'd said those haunting words—the last he'd spoken.

"I don't know. I left the CIA before I heard the results." She considered the possibility Trevor might still be alive. The thought was crippling. One of their own had been responsible for taking out their entire team because he knew David had seen him and could bring him up on charges. Trevor had been hunting her ever since because he believed David shared his suspicions with her.

"I can't believe it." But David's words played through her mind. *It's our own people.*

David's phone was so badly damaged that it wouldn't make a call. She replaced the battery to Ethan's phone and called the number she'd seen on David's for his friend Wes. "No answer. I don't like it. I'm calling Robert. He should know about this new development. And I want to make sure he received the pictures."

"Do it. Call him now," Aaron said with a grave look on his face.

She dialed Robert's number again. He answered on the first ring.

"Are you okay? Has something else happened?"

"No, nothing has happened, but I have information for you. Did you get the photos I sent you?"

"I did. I have no idea who the other men are, but I've identified the one you called Mike Logan. He was stationed at Bagram, but get this, he's been AWOL for over a year now."

"You're kidding." Victoria's head swam. She paused for a moment, then told him about the video and what they suspected about Trevor.

Robert's silence was lengthy. "Trevor was one of my best people," he said quietly. "I trusted him completely. I can't imagine him being involved in such a thing."

"Was his body recovered?" She put the phone on speaker so that they all could hear the conversation.

"I'm afraid the blast burned so hot we weren't able to recover any bodies."

"Did David ever mention contacting his friend Wes Sorenson to you?" She told Robert about the photos David sent his friend.

"No, he never mentioned the man." Robert paused. "If this is Trevor, he'll do his best to make sure you don't walk out of there alive. And anyone else who stands in his way." He huffed out a breath. "We have no idea how widespread this conspiracy really is. Trevor could have others within the agency working for him. Are you all safe for now?"

"Yes, I think so. I'm guessing they were able to locate me through you. They've probably been tracking your calls."

"Probably, but you were smart to call my burner phone. We can speak freely."

"I'm so glad you kept it, but we don't have much time, Robert. They have men all over the area. They'll find this location soon enough." She pulled in a breath. "David suspected Trevor of something and followed him to one of the locations in the photos. That's what he meant when he said it's our own people."

"This is all so unbelievable," Robert said. "Stay where you are. My men will be in touch on this number when they reach the area, which will be soon. Until then, hang tight and stay out of sight. And if you spot Trevor's men, call me right away. Stay safe, Victoria." Robert ended the call.

Victoria held onto a small amount of comfort in knowing Robert was sending men he trusted to bring them in. Would they arrive too late?

"We can't let down our guard for a moment. These men have everything to lose if they are exposed. I say we take shifts sweeping the property. We can't afford any more surprise attacks." Ethan glanced around the room. "Jim and I will take the first shift. I'll ask Harrison to come as well. Keep the phone here with you, Victoria, in case Robert calls back with more information. In the meantime, you should try and get some rest. Both of you." He glanced at Aaron. "You look beat."

"I will go with you," Fletcher offered. "This is a large place and you will need much help." He turned to Hunter. "Come with us?"

"No, let me," Aaron said.

Fletcher shook his head. "*Bruder,* you are in no shape to be doing anything. Rest. We'll be fine."

With so many things unsettled, Victoria couldn't sit quietly by and do nothing. She went to the window and watched as the men disappeared around the side of the barn.

Why hadn't she seen this coming? Why hadn't David shared his concerns with her? If only she'd known the truth before that final mission. Perhaps the outcome would be different and David and the others wouldn't have sacrificed their lives for people with greed in their hearts.

Mamm brought coffee over and handed him a cup. "Though I wish you would try to sleep."

Aaron shook his head. "I'm *oke. Denki* for the coffee." Aaron sipped the strong black liquid and its warm steam tickled his nose. As much as his body desired sleep, he couldn't relax until he knew the threat had passed.

"I have some for Victoria, too. I'm sure she could use a boost." Aaron followed his mother's gaze to where Victoria stood guard by the window.

"Let me." He took the coffee from her without missing the look his *mamm* gave him. He could see she had questions. He wasn't ready to talk about what he felt with her or anyone.

Victoria looked his way as he came near. He held out the cup to her.

"Thank you," she murmured with a smile.

"Do you see something out there?" He nodded toward the window and she shook her head.

"No. I guess that's a good thing." She didn't sound so sure.

He noticed she held one of the photos in her hand. "Have you discovered anything new there?" No matter how hard he tried, Aaron couldn't dismiss the feeling that there were many pieces missing still.

"I'm not sure. This man standing off to the right of Logan… He has his back to the camera, and yet there is something familiar about him—about his stance. I wish I could get a better look at him."

Aaron took the photo from her and studied the man. "I don't recognize him as any of the men who have been coming after us."

"Me, either, but I was hoping." She sipped the coffee. "I have a bad feeling, Aaron. I can't shake it."

He set down his coffee cup on the windowsill and turned her to face him. "What has you so worried?" he asked gently.

She stared into his eyes. The lost look on her face tugged at his heartstrings.

"I don't know. I feel as if I'm missing something important." She heaved a heavy sigh. "I want this to be over. I want..." She didn't finish and he longed to ask what she wished for.

Aaron glanced around the room only to realize it was just the two of them. Quiet conversation drifted out from the kitchen into the living room. The evening meal was being prepared this Christmas Eve. Normally they would be getting together at his family home for the holiday. Would they be able to celebrate this most sacred holiday? Would they all still be alive?

"It will be soon. You can't give up hope. *Gott* is watching out for us."

She couldn't hide her doubts. "I want to believe that, but I feel as if I've let David down by not figuring this out sooner. If only I'd asked him what was wrong. I knew something was troubling him, but I thought…"

Aaron touched her cheek. She closed her eyes for a moment and leaned into his hand.

"You are doing what you can to right this wrong. You can't blame yourself for these men's actions."

She reached for his hand and held it between hers, a smile lifting the corners of her mouth. "Thank you, Aaron."

More than anything he wanted it to end for her. After what she'd gone through, Victoria deserved to have some happiness in her life. Yet when he thought about what that might look like, he couldn't see her staying in West Kootenai. Where did that leave them?

Her eyes grew dark and she stepped closer. He pulled in a shaky breath and cupped her face between his hands. He had no right to want a future with her. No right. Yet he did.

"Victoria…" Her name slipped from his lips. She closed the inches between them and kissed him fervently, and all his doubts disappeared.

There were many things he would regret when she was gone, but for the moment, he would let himself care for this special woman, and he would hold that love in his heart for the rest of his life.

A noise nearby filtered through his drumming heartbeat. A door opened and slammed against the wall. Aaron jerked toward the sound.

Ethan was the first inside. "There are men moving around on the adjoining property. I don't think they saw us, but it was close."

Jim and Harrison, along with Aaron's brothers, rushed in and shut the door quickly.

Victoria ducked away from the window and pulled Aaron with her. "How many?"

"We couldn't be sure." Fletcher looked to his brother.

"At least a dozen," Hunter said. "They appeared to be heading away from this place, but still."

If there were that many men at the neighbor's property, how many more were out there closing in on them?

"They don't know we're here." Victoria rubbed a hand across her forehead. "I'm going to try to reach Robert again. This can't wait."

She dialed the number and frowned. "The signal's gone."

"That's strange. It was working a little while ago. Usually the signal's pretty good in this area." Jim tried his. "I can't get a signal, either." He looked at Victoria.

"Maybe they're blocking it." Her chilling words hung in the air between them while Aaron's mind struggled to understand how that was possible.

"We can't sit here and wait for them to come to us. Not after what happened the last time." Aaron looked to Victoria for support. "It's time to leave while we still can."

She didn't hesitate. "Aaron's right. We can't risk all these people's lives."

"Copy that." Ethan moved to the door. "Between the two vehicles we should be able to fit everyone. Let's get to them. We'll figure the rest out once we're rolling."

Martha went to the kitchen and turned off the stove, removing the casserole from the oven. "It's a shame we have to leave it here."

Holding Caleb's hand in his, Aaron ushered his *mamm* out the door and looked around for Victoria.

"*Mamm,* you go with Hunter and Fletcher in the SUV. There'll be more room there. Victoria, Caleb, and I will ride with Jim in his truck." He looked down at his *sohn*. "Help me with the barn door."

Aaron unhooked the board that kept the two doors secured and threw one open, while Caleb did the same with the second.

Darkness covered the land. Snow had begun to drizzle again. It was Christmas Eve, but there was no peace to be found anywhere in his heart. Certainly not in his community.

Ethan ushered as many people as he could fit into the SUV before leaving the barn. Once both vehicles were clear, Aaron secured the doors and climbed in the truck next to his *sohn* and Victoria.

With Jim behind the wheel, they pulled in behind Ethan as he eased toward the road. Aaron kept his eyes on the tree-lined path visible through the vehicle's headlights. The ammunition was almost gone. If they were attacked again, would anyone survive?

Victoria tried the cell phone again. "Still no response." Her troubled gaze held Aaron's, sending him a message. She believed the lack of service was no accident.

As they turned onto the road, Aaron struggled to come up with somewhere they could stay safe until Victoria's commander came for them.

"What are we going to do?" Caleb's frightened eyes latched onto his father's, seeking assurances Aaron couldn't give.

"I don't know, *sohn*, but we'll figure it out. Don't worry."

"Heads up. There are a couple of vehicles coming our way," Jim warned, capturing everyone's attention.

Two sets of headlights topped the hill in front of them.

"Whatever you do, don't stop. Aaron, get as low as possible. Caleb, you, too. If it's them, they'll recognize us." Victoria leaned over in the seat until she was no longer visible. Aaron and Caleb followed her example.

Jim kept his speed slow and steady as the first vehicle drew up beside him. The second was only a few feet off the car's bumper.

"They're past us now," Jim told them. "I counted at least four men in the first vehicle. Probably the same in the second."

Aaron sat up and looked behind them in time to see both cars hit their brakes. "They're stopping."

Jim flashed his lights several times. As if in answer, Ethan hit the gas and the SUV sped out in front of them while Jim responded in the same manner.

"I sure hope Ethan has a plan," Jim murmured as he pushed the truck to its limit.

Suddenly, Ethan killed his lights.

"What's he doing?" Aaron asked.

"He's trying to keep those men from seeing which way we're going," Victoria told him as Jim did the same. The SUV swung onto a small gravel road off to the right. "Any idea where this road leads?"

Aaron struggled with the layout of the land outside of the community. "There are only a few Amish farms this direction." One that he knew for certain. "Jonah's grandparents live down this way."

Ethan turned onto the side road that would eventually lead to their farm while Aaron kept watch behind him. The two sets of headlights flashed onto the same road they'd left. "They're still coming."

In front of them, Ethan suddenly jerked the SUV off the road. Without either vehicle's headlights, it was hard to see the tree-filled space in front of them.

The occupants of the truck braced as Jim followed.

"He's hiding since we can't outrun them. Hopefully, they'll blow right past us without ever spotting our tracks leaving the road," Victoria said and held onto the seat tight to keep from bouncing off it.

Neither Jim nor Ethan stopped until they'd gone some ways into the woods.

"Let's hope this works," Jim said, huffing out the tense words. "Because if not, there's no way we can escape them on foot."

"If we have to hike out from here, where will this direction lead us?" Victoria pointed straight ahead of them.

"Eventually to Jonah's grandparents' place." But the hike wouldn't be easy.

"I see their headlights." Jim watched his side mirror closely. Two vehicles flew down the road past them.

Aaron held his breath and expected the drivers to tap their brakes at any moment. When they didn't, he exhaled.

"I can't believe they missed our tracks," Victoria said as she watched the taillights of the two vehicles disappear.

"Me, either." Aaron noticed Ethan heading their way and got out along with the others.

"I heard car doors shutting up ahead," Ethan told them. "There's a real chance they may have seen where we went off the road and are waiting for us to emerge. Which means they've probably radioed for backup to cut us off. We're running out of options." He glanced between them all.

Victoria tried the cell phone again. "Still no service. I don't think we have a choice. They'll hear the engines if we try to drive. There's only one way. We have to hike out."

SEVENTEEN

She'd been fighting so hard to stay alive, and yet the enemy kept throwing everything they had her way. There were more innocent lives at stake now, and she couldn't let anything happen to them.

"There's the house," Jonah said. Through the trees, candles glowed in the windows of a small house. Relief threatened to drop her to her knees. Only a few more steps, and yet it looked like a mile.

The long hike hadn't been an easy one for Aaron's mother or Caleb. And poor Ruth. Victoria couldn't imagine how difficult it was to walk through the wilderness in the dark and cold while being pregnant. Harrison had kept a close watch over his wife throughout the journey. They'd stopped frequently to rest.

Now that they reached the clearing between the house and woods, Victoria grabbed Aaron's arm and stopped. Paranoia had her second-guessing everything.

She turned her face up to him. "What if they're waiting for us inside?" After what they'd been through, she couldn't discount the possibility.

He smiled gently and took her hand. "Then we will face it together." He'd never once wavered in his support of her, even when it had to seem unwise. She couldn't fall apart on him now.

With Aaron holding her hand, she stepped into the clearing. Nothing happened. The rest of their weary group followed them to the porch, where Jonah knocked on his grandparents' door.

Seconds ticked by while Victoria's eyes darted around the darkness looking for trouble.

An older man opened the door and stepped back in surprise when the lantern picked up the number of people on his porch.

"*Grossdaddi*, it's me." Jonah leaned in enough for the man to confirm his identity.

"Jonah." A smile spread across his weathered face. "Has something happened?"

"*Jah*, it has. May we come inside?"

The man scanned the faces around him before he stepped back to let them all in. A slender woman around his age clung to his side.

"*Grossmammi.*" Jonah hugged her and did

his best to explain what they'd gone through. "Have either of you seen anyone around the place tonight?"

"Nay." The older man confirmed with a shake of his head. "Not a stir."

Victoria tried the phone once more. No signal. Somehow the phones were being blocked and she had no way to reach Robert.

She grabbed Aaron's attention and stepped outside with him. "The phone still isn't working. Without it, Robert has no way of reaching out to us and I feel as if they're closing in. We no longer have a choice. We need to go to the sheriff and explain what happened. Perhaps he can reach Robert." As bad as she hated trusting anyone, this was way out of their control. "The only question is how? We left our vehicles in the woods. We can't go back for them."

"Jonah's Grandfather Isaac has an enclosed buggy. I'm sure he will let us use it."

As she looked into his eyes, she wished for so many things. All impossible because of her past. "Let me do this alone, Aaron. Please."

He stepped closer, his piercing eyes filled with…love? Love for her? Victoria's heart broke. Hope died. Reality came crashing in. She did not deserve his love.

She started past him before he could see the pain, but he caught her arm and drew her close.

As she looked into his handsome face, she gave in to her heart's desire and closed the space between them. Victoria framed his face with her hands and kissed him with all her heart. She loved him so much, but was it enough to let him go? That decision was for another time. Right now, she just wanted to keep on kissing him and shut out the truth waiting beyond this nightmare. It was impossible to rewrite her past. Aaron deserved so much better—a good woman to share his life with. Someone deserving of his love. Someone other than her.

Victoria pulled free and turned away. Her hand covered her swollen lips. Tears blinded her eyes.

The silence between them stretched out uncomfortably. She bit her bottom lip hard to hold back the pain.

"I will ask Isaac about the buggy." His tone was sharp. She'd hurt him badly. "But I am going with you." The door opened, but she couldn't look at him. He shut it hard behind him and Victoria fought back tears. She'd fallen in love with a man who could never be hers.

Time passed slowly while she tried to get control over her breaking heart.

The door opened once more. She scrubbed her face with both hands and slowly faced Aaron's rigid frame haloed by the flashlight's beam.

"Isaac gave us permission to use the buggy. We'll have to stay off the roads, but I know a path we can take that will keep us out of sight. Are you ready?"

Victoria slowly nodded and followed him to the barn.

They worked quickly to harness a horse to the buggy. Once on board, Aaron eased from the barn.

"The box of evidence," Victoria exclaimed, panicked she'd forgotten it inside.

Aaron patted the front of his jacket where he'd tucked it inside. "Don't worry. I have it."

She faced forward and couldn't stop shaking. From the cold? Or her own doubts?

"Here, this will keep you warm." Aaron placed a heavy quilt across her lap.

Despite her heart breaking, she smiled. "Thank you." She was hanging on by a thread emotionally. Above all else, she had to finish this final mission once and for all.

A strain remained between them as they headed for the town of Eagle's Nest, where the sheriff's department was located. Throughout the drive, she couldn't relax.

"We are almost to the road that will lead us into town." Aaron didn't look her way as he spoke.

She stared up at the falling snow. A year ago,

on Christmas Eve, she never would have pictured herself here. The West Kootenai community beckoned her home. Her weary soul longed for this life. No matter what, she'd find her place in the sun. There would be no more time spent in the dark world of espionage for her. And maybe in time, she'd forget about this man at her side who made her believe in the impossible again.

Up ahead something dark blocked the path. Victoria leaned forward. "What is that?"

Aaron pulled on the reins and the horse stopped. "It appears a tree has fallen across the road. Probably the weight of the snow and ice was too much for it." Yet there was doubt in his tone.

He jumped down and headed over to the obstacle. Victoria went with him. The tree spread across the entire road. Aaron kneeled beside it and something in his face alarmed her.

"What's wrong?" Then she noticed. This had nothing to do with the snow or ice. The tree had been deliberately cut, probably with a chainsaw.

The noise of engines interrupted her frantic pulse as one thought became clear.

They'd been found.

"Run, Victoria." Together, they raced for the buggy, but there was not enough time. Soon, they were surrounded by vehicles. Armed men poured out. One man grabbed Aaron and restrained him.

"Aaron!" Victoria screamed and tried to run to him. Someone grabbed her from behind and held her tight.

Tears filled her eyes. She struggled to free herself, but the man holding her forced her toward one of the waiting cars.

"Take care of him." The voice of the man holding her threatened to take away all hope. "Get in, Victoria. It's time to finish this once and for all."

Trevor Hawk forced her to face him, a sick smile on his face.

"How could you do this to your own people?" She tried to break free, but he held her in a vise grip.

"You're not going anywhere but in an unmarked grave somewhere. It's finished, Victoria." The enemy had been hiding among their own all along. Trevor was Robert's second in command.

"Get in." Trevor shoved her hard toward the opened door and she stumbled inside.

A gunshot resounded from near where Aaron had been restrained.

The tears fell from her eyes. She struggled to keep from losing it completely.

Another man waited inside. As her eyes

adjusted to the dark interior, her world collapsed. There would be no help coming for her or Aaron. The man seated there was her former CIA commander, Robert Jamison. Robert wasn't the man of honor she believed him to be. He was the one behind the whole conspiracy and probably the person responsible for ordering David's death.

"So you figured it out. You were never supposed to live long enough to realize my involvement. If it hadn't been for all the mistakes made in getting rid of you, my being here would have been unnecessary." He glanced at Trevor with distaste. "But I could no longer leave something this critical to anyone but myself."

He was speaking as if he was merely talking about a mission and not about eliminating her.

"Why?" She forced the word out on a ragged sob. "Was it all because you were afraid to get caught smuggling heroin?" She had to know. If she was going to die, she had to know the truth.

"Heroin?" Robert scoffed in surprise. "This has nothing to do with drugs."

Shocked, Victoria stared at him as the truth finally became clear. "It wasn't heroin you were moving. It was something else…" She tried to recall what Robert told her about Logan. He was stationed at Bagram, had gone AWOL.

The answer finally registered. "Logan was

the one responsible for delivering the weapons that the Pentagon had earmarked for the Afghan security forces." She remembered David talking about the weapons that were being distributed to the Afghan soldiers. It made sense that was Logan's connection to all of this. He'd have access to the weapons. Could manipulate the records.

"With his help, you were selling some of them." She saw the truth in Robert's eyes as she untangled the last bit. She lunged for him, but Trevor grabbed her arms. "You were, weren't you? You're a traitor. You killed David to keep your crime secret. All for greed."

Robert stared at her without feeling. "So you finally figured out the truth. Well, I guess it doesn't matter now. You'll be dead soon enough. Like your Amish hero. Yes, Logan oversaw the receipt of weapons from the Pentagon. He kept half and distributed the rest to the Afghan security forces. It was a lucrative business for us all. Logan made the arrangements to sell the weapons on the black market to whatever organization offered the most money. We split the profit. Everyone was happy, and the Pentagon had no idea, thanks to bad record keeping. Until David stuck his nose where it didn't belong." His voice was filled with hatred.

"He snuck into one of the camps where we

were keeping the weapons. He saw Logan meeting with some of the people he was selling the weapons to. David managed to photograph the ledger before he was spotted by Logan and got away. The ledger contained serial numbers for each weapon we were selling. Of course, it only showed the number part of the serial. Any identification of the weapons manufacturer was left off deliberately in case the ledger fell into the wrong hands. Like David's. I knew it was only a matter of time before he figured out the truth. He was too good at what he did."

Robert stared out the window as he continued. "David came to me once he'd identified Logan. He told me he started following Logan's movements and caught him with Trevor. I asked him to let me handle it and he agreed. I knew I had to get rid of David before he blabbed to someone higher up than me. So I concocted a fake mission. David had no idea what was in store until it was too late to alert anyone, or so I thought."

But David had alerted someone. Her. He'd left that message.

"You all were supposed to die." Robert faced her with the devastating news, as if he was merely discussing something unpleasant instead of arranging the murders of multiple CIA agents. "I couldn't take the chance David hadn't shared his discovery with you or one of the other agents."

He pinned her with a look that sent a shiver down her spine. "And you went and got that poor Amish man involved in your problems. Because of your foolishness, he's dead." Her stomach turned at the way Robert smirked.

Please, God, no!

"How could you kill David? He looked up to you. We both did." Tears choked her voice.

At that, Robert finally showed some regret. "I cared for him, as well, but I had no choice. He was going to ruin everything." Robert shifted in his seat. "Now, you will tell me where the evidence is hidden. We can make this easy or excruciatingly painful. It's up to you."

Through her frantic thoughts, another piece of the puzzle fell into place. The man whose stance appeared familiar in one of those pictures—it was Robert. David hadn't figured out that part yet. Bile rose in her throat at how easy Robert had betrayed someone who came to him for help. He'd trusted Robert to help him bring down dirty agents. And in the end, it had cost him his life.

A horse whinnied somewhere in the fog of his mind. Aaron slowly opened his eyes. Sharp pains in his chest shot spasms through his side.

He'd been shot. The fog lifted. The attack. Victoria. He sat up and grabbed his chest. Remembering the metal box of evidence he'd stuck inside his jacket, Aaron pulled it out. A bullet had lodged in the box, saving his life. All *Gott's* doing. He'd passed out. The men had probably assumed the shot to the chest would be fatal and had left. And it would have been if it weren't for the box.

Aaron stumbled to his feet. The buggy was where he'd left it, but the cars were gone. They'd taken Victoria. He grabbed one end of the tree and heaved, but he was much too weak to budge it.

He climbed onto the seat and shook the reins, guiding the horse into the shallow ditch. The animal slowly climbed up the opposite side and into deep snow while Aaron struggled not to pass out.

The going was slow and took time he couldn't afford to lose. Once he cleared where the tree was, he urged the horse back down and onto the road. All Aaron could think about was that Victoria was in danger.

The first of the shops came into view. The holiday decorations lining Main Street twinkled brightly. It was past midnight, so now Christmas Day. The town was all but deserted.

Aaron spotted the sheriff's station and pulled the buggy up front.

Dismounting, he staggered inside the station to where two deputies and a man dressed as a civilian watched a TV screen.

All stood at his arrival.

The man in civilian clothes rushed toward Aaron. "Are you okay?"

"She's in danger," he said, barely managing to get the words out. "Please, help me."

Another man emerged from the office. "I'm Sheriff Collins. What's going on?"

Aaron did his best to explain what had happened. "They have her and she's in danger. They'll kill her."

The sheriff didn't hesitate. "Do you have any idea where they would take her?"

Aaron could think of only one place. He told the sheriff about Victoria's cabin.

The sheriff clamped his arm. "Stay here where it's warm—"

Aaron didn't wait for him to finish. "I'm going with you. She needs me."

"That's not going to happen. You're a civilian," the sheriff insisted.

"I'm going with you."

Sheriff Collins stared at him for a long moment before he agreed. "All right. Call in the rest of the team," he told the older man. "Have them meet us there. Tell them to go in silent. And get in touch with this Robert Jamison. Find out what we're up against." While the dispatcher went to work, the sheriff addressed his two deputies. "Ryan, you and Aden follow me. Aaron, you'll ride in my cruiser." Sheriff Collins headed out the back door to his patrol car and Aaron followed. The two deputies climbed into another vehicle and they all headed out of town.

All Aaron could think about was Victoria. What if he was wrong and the men had left the area entirely? Victoria could be dead already.

No, please, no.

"You said these men are CIA?" Sheriff Collins shot Aaron a questioning look.

"I'm not sure if they all are, but some are CIA." Aaron understood how far-fetched his story sounded. He was glad the sheriff appeared to believe him. "The man in charge is supposed to be dead." He told Sheriff Collins about the mission where Victoria's partner and team perished.

"Unbelievable." Collins focused on the road ahead. "There is more to the story than what we know, I guarantee it."

Aaron had no doubt. As he stared at the dark countryside, he prayed for Victoria's safety.

Whether she would accept it or not, he loved her and wanted to share his life with her.

"There are my people." Collins's voice intruded into Aaron's thoughts. The sheriff pulled off the road and stopped.

"Sheriff, you copy?" The dispatcher's voice came through the radio and Collins snatched up the mic.

"I'm here, Bernie. What'd you find out?"

"Something strange. Apparently, Jamison hasn't been in the office for a while. No one knows where he's at."

Aaron whipped toward the sheriff. "What does that mean?"

Collins ended the transmission. "I have no idea, but you are to stay here, where it's safe. Understood?" He eyed Aaron with a stern look.

"No, not understood. I'm coming with you. I can't let anything happen to her." His voice broke as he thought about losing Victoria.

"You're staying here. Don't make me put you in handcuffs."

Aaron couldn't let that happen. He gave in. "*Oke*, I'll wait in the vehicle."

Collins looked him in the eye for a long moment before slowly nodding.

The sheriff stepped out and headed to his men. After a quick discussion, they traipsed into the woods while Aaron was left to wait and wonder.

Seconds ticked off in time with his heartbeat while his fear continued to grow. Multiple gunshots sounded in the woods, and Aaron jumped from the vehicle.

Something out of the corner of his eye grabbed his attention. He turned in time to see a man he didn't recognize dragging Victoria from the woods toward one of the deputy's vehicles. If he escaped, she'd be dead.

"Stop!" Aaron yelled.

The man whirled toward Aaron with his gun drawn. Victoria managed to free herself and scrambled for the gun in the man's hand. He swung the weapon and it struck her with a glancing blow. Victoria fell to her knees. The man aimed the weapon at her with his finger on the trigger.

"No!" Aaron dove and slammed against the man's body. A shot split the air above him. Victoria screamed and grabbed her shoulder. Blood quickly covered her shirt.

Voices carried through the woods. The sheriff and his men were coming.

Aaron grabbed the man and struggled to get the weapon away, but he wasn't about to go down without a fight. He slugged Aaron hard.

Before the man could strike him again, two deputies pulled him off and cuffed him.

Victoria. She'd been shot. He scrambled over to where she was lying and kneeled down.

"I'm okay," she quickly assured him with a smile. "I've been through much worse."

More deputies exited the woods with men in cuffs, but all Aaron could think about was this wounded woman he loved.

"Ambulance is here." The sheriff stopped beside them. "Let them take a look at you."

Victoria sat up slowly as two EMTs rushed to assist her.

While she was being treated, another vehicle pulled up next to the sheriff's cruiser.

Several men in suits headed toward them. Victoria staggered to her feet and almost lost her footing. Aaron reached for her arm. "Who are these men?" he asked when she appeared to recognize them.

"One is the director of the CIA."

While Aaron struggled to grasp the meaning, the man she indicated as the director stopped beside her.

"Victoria." The man extended his hand. "Glad to see you on two feet. May I have a word?"

Victoria followed him a little ways away while Aaron waited.

Her conversation with the director was brief.

When he'd finished, he headed to where the sheriff and his people were gathered.

Victoria waited until they'd left before she joined Aaron again.

"What did he want?" he asked, his full attention on her face. He loved her, but he wouldn't hold her back from finding her happiness.

"He told me Ethan's decoder friend reached out to him. Turns out they know each other. Ethan's friend figured out the list was serial numbers of weapons that were shipped by the Pentagon to the Afghan security forces." She shared what she'd learned from Robert about his crimes.

She stopped and held Aaron's gaze. "And he offered me my old job back." She waited for him to say something, but how could he when each word was like a knife to his heart.

"So you will be leaving now that this is finished?"

She stepped closer, her eyes shining with something he hoped was love.

"No, Aaron, I told you I'm done with that life." She took his hands in hers. "But there are some things you must know about me, things I've done in the name of justice." He held his breath while she struggled to get the words out. "I'm not a good person. I've killed before. Many times." Victoria laid her heart bare. Told him all the terrible things she was responsible for in her past. "But I'm finished with the *Englisch* world. I plan to return to the Amish way of life and…" She stopped. Pulled in a breath. "And I love you, Aaron. But I don't deserve you or—"

Aaron stopped her. "I love you, too. And you deserve only *gut* things."

Tears filled her eyes. "I want to believe you."

"Then do. You are not the bad things you did, Victoria. That's not who you are. I love you and want to share my life with you, but I want you to be sure about your decision. After so many years away from the Plain life, will you be happy living it again?" He had to know, couldn't bear the thought of her regretting her decision.

A smile that he'd never seen before lit up her face and she kissed him. "More than happy. This is the life I've wanted for so long and I will be happy to share it with you and Caleb." Above them, the stars broke free of the clouds almost as if they were a guiding light to bring her home again.

"This is the best Christmas ever." She hugged him close. "I thought I'd never be able to return to this life. Through all the dangerous things I've faced, I didn't think it possible to come back home to my Amish roots, but with *Gott* all things are possible." She smiled up at him.

"There are no more shadow games. No more anger or guilt. Just the love I have for you. The life we'll build together. And I will spend the rest of my life trying to be worthy of your love."

He smiled at the woman who had changed his life for the better. "Our future will not be defined by the past, but by what we make of it together. And it will be a good one because we love each other with all our hearts."

EPILOGUE

Six weeks later

"That must be him," Victoria said as a blond man walked across the frozen ground of the cemetery toward them. She reached for Aaron's hand for strength. This was the first time she'd been away from the West Kootenai community since she'd shed the trappings of her old life and her heart had soared without restraints into the simple Plain world.

The weight of her past no longer held her back, all because of the man at her side. Aaron had been her rock. He'd risked his life for her. She'd spend the rest of hers trying to be the best *fraa* and *mamm* she could be for him and for Caleb.

Aaron hadn't once wavered in his love for her, and she would work hard to relearn the simple ways. She'd met with the bishop. News of what happened had spread throughout the West Kootenai community. The people had welcomed her into the biweekly church service…and into Aaron's family.

In time, she and Aaron would marry, but there was work to be done first.

As the man neared them, his eyes widened at Victoria's Amish clothing and she smiled.

"Wes Sorenson?" she asked. This would be the first time she'd met David's childhood friend.

"Yes," he said at last. "I'm sorry. Ethan didn't mention you were Amish." Ethan had been kind enough to track down Wes for her. She wanted to thank him for helping David. She'd learned Wes had no idea David was dead.

She shook his hand and turned to Aaron. "This is Aaron Shetler."

"Nice to meet you." Wes nodded to Aaron, then faced Victoria once more. "I still can't believe he's gone."

Victoria's heart went out to him. She'd had a year to adjust. "I'm so sorry, but I can't thank you enough for what you did. We wouldn't have figured out who was responsible for David's death without you."

Wes turned to the headstone of his friend. "He was a true hero. When we finished our tour of duty, I couldn't wait to get out of the army, but not David. He reenlisted and served another tour. Then he joined the CIA."

Victoria smiled. "You're right. He was a hero."

"I was scared to death when those men came to my house and wanted to know what David gave me. I had no idea what was going on, but it scared me enough to send me into hiding in Alaska. Turns out, it was the best thing to happen to me. I love living there." He shook his head. "I tried to reach out to David, but he never called back. I wish I'd known." Wes fought back tears.

Victoria clasped his arm. "I'm sorry for your loss, but I have something David would want you to have." She handed Wes the lighter and David's old phone. The CIA had gone through the phone and found more information that would seal Robert and Trevor's fates, along with those of many others. The people responsible for the deaths of David and the rest of the team would pay the ultimate price for their treason.

"The lighter belonged to David's grandfather. You probably knew him. The phone has pictures of David that I thought you might like to keep." She'd always love David, but it was time to let him go and move toward the future. Holding onto pieces of the past would only make that hard.

Wes fingered the lighter. "I do remember him. David loved this. Thank you." He hugged her briefly then stared into her eyes. Being with someone else who had loved David as much as she had was healing.

"You're welcome." She managed to get out the words past the lump in her throat. "Where will you go now? Will you stay in Alaska?"

He smiled. "Yeah, I kind of like living there. It's peaceful, and I met someone. We're getting married." He glanced to Aaron. "Looks like you did, too. I'm glad. David talked about you a lot. He'd want you to be happy. He wouldn't want you to be sad forever."

Tears stung her eyes and she nodded because getting words out was almost impossible.

"Goodbye, Victoria." Wes hugged her again. "Be happy." He shook Aaron's hand, then turned to touch the headstone one more time before he headed across the cemetery to his car.

"Can you give me a moment?" Victoria turned to the man who held her heart and her future.

Aaron slowly nodded and kissed her cheek. He started toward the Amish taxi they'd hired for this trip to Colorado.

"It's over, David," she whispered. He would always hold a piece of her heart. "You can rest now. Thanks to you, we finally know the truth. You saved so many lives."

She touched the headstone and placed the flowers she'd bought into the stone vase.

"I'll always love you," she whispered with

a catch in her throat. "I have a chance at happiness with someone who doesn't understand our old way of life, and for that I'm grateful." She placed a photo on the headstone of her and David along with their team who had died, making sure Trevor was not part of it. He didn't deserve to rest with David.

After a final look, she turned toward the future and spotted Aaron—the man who had made the trip to Colorado with her. The one who had gone with her to St. Ignatius to visit her *mamm* and *daed's* graves. Thanks to Aaron, she'd been reconnected with the couple who'd cared for her after her mother's passing, and with so many others in the community who loved her family.

With her heart filled with happiness, she headed across the uneven ground to his side, her eyes shining with love.

For the first time in a long time, she wasn't looking at the past and its mistakes. She was keeping her focus firmly on the future with Aaron and his son.

Victoria went into his arms and hugged him tight, so grateful to this man who had saved her from herself.

* * * * *

*If you enjoyed this story,
don't miss Mary Alford's next
Amish romantic suspense,
available next year from
Love Inspired Suspense!*

*Find more great reads at
www.LoveInspired.com*

Dear Reader,

Thank you for taking this trip with me to the beautiful Amish community of West Kootenai, Montana. I hope you have enjoyed Victoria and Aaron's journey to find happiness after facing so much darkness. I loved watching their brokenness heal as love blooms where only guilt and hopelessness existed before. Their story touched my heart. I hope it did yours, as well.

Stories of redemption have always been a favorite of mine. I love it when two people finally let go of their mistakes and accept the promises God has in store for them. Though letting go of the past is sometimes hard, if we trust God, He will turn our ashes into beauty. What an amazing promise!

God bless,
Mary Alford

Get 4 FREE REWARDS!

We'll send you 2 FREE Books plus 2 FREE Mystery Gifts.

Love Inspired books feature uplifting stories where faith helps guide you through life's challenges and discover the promise of a new beginning.

FREE Value Over $20

YES! Please send me 2 FREE Love Inspired Romance novels and my 2 FREE mystery gifts (gifts are worth about $10 retail). After receiving them, if I don't wish to receive any more books, I can return the shipping statement marked "cancel." If I don't cancel, I will receive 6 brand-new novels every month and be billed just $5.24 each for the regular-print edition or $5.99 each for the larger-print edition in the U.S., or $5.74 each for the regular-print edition or $6.24 each for the larger-print edition in Canada. That's a savings of at least 13% off the cover price. It's quite a bargain! Shipping and handling is just 50¢ per book in the U.S. and $1.25 per book in Canada.* I understand that accepting the 2 free books and gifts places me under no obligation to buy anything. I can always return a shipment and cancel at any time. The free books and gifts are mine to keep no matter what I decide.

Choose one: ☐ **Love Inspired Romance Regular-Print** (105/305 IDN GNWC)   ☐ **Love Inspired Romance Larger-Print** (122/322 IDN GNWC)

Name (please print)

Address   Apt. #

City   State/Province   Zip/Postal Code

Email: Please check this box ☐ if you would like to receive newsletters and promotional emails from Harlequin Enterprises ULC and its affiliates. You can unsubscribe anytime.

Mail to the Reader Service:
IN U.S.A.: P.O. Box 1341, Buffalo, NY 14240-8531
IN CANADA: P.O. Box 603, Fort Erie, Ontario L2A 5X3

Want to try 2 free books from another series? Call 1-800-873-8635 or visit www.ReaderService.com.

---

*Terms and prices subject to change without notice. Prices do not include sales taxes, which will be charged (if applicable) based on your state or country of residence. Canadian residents will be charged applicable taxes. Offer not valid in Quebec. This offer is limited to one order per household. Books received may not be as shown. Not valid for current subscribers to Love Inspired Romance books. All orders subject to approval. Credit or debit balances in a customer's account(s) may be offset by any other outstanding balance owed by or to the customer. Please allow 4 to 6 weeks for delivery. Offer available while quantities last.

Your Privacy—Your information is being collected by Harlequin Enterprises ULC, operating as Reader Service. For a complete summary of the information we collect, how we use this information and to whom it is disclosed, please visit our privacy notice located at corporate.harlequin.com/privacy-notice. From time to time we may also exchange your personal information with reputable third parties. If you wish to opt out of this sharing of your personal information, please visit readerservice.com/consumerchoice or call 1-800-873-8635. **Notice to California Residents**—Under California law, you have specific rights to control and access your data. For more information on these rights and how to exercise them, visit corporate.harlequin.com/california-privacy.

LI20R2

Get 4 FREE REWARDS!

We'll send you 2 FREE Books plus 2 FREE Mystery Gifts.

Harlequin Heartwarming Larger-Print books will connect you to uplifting stories where the bonds of friendship, family and community unite.

FREE
Value Over
$20

YES! Please send me 2 FREE Harlequin Heartwarming Larger-Print novels and my 2 FREE mystery gifts (gifts worth about $10 retail). After receiving them, if I don't wish to receive any more books, I can return the shipping statement marked "cancel." If I don't cancel, I will receive 4 brand-new larger-print novels every month and be billed just $5.74 per book in the U.S. or $6.24 per book in Canada. That's a savings of at least 21% off the cover price. It's quite a bargain! Shipping and handling is just 50¢ per book in the U.S. and $1.25 per book in Canada.* I understand that accepting the 2 free books and gifts places me under no obligation to buy anything. I can always return a shipment and cancel at any time. The free books and gifts are mine to keep no matter what I decide.

161/361 HDN GNPZ

Name (please print)

Address   Apt. #

City   State/Province   Zip/Postal Code

Email: Please check this box ☐ if you would like to receive newsletters and promotional emails from Harlequin Enterprises ULC and its affiliates. You can unsubscribe anytime.

Mail to the **Reader Service:**
IN U.S.A.: P.O. Box 1341, Buffalo, NY 14240-8531
IN CANADA: P.O. Box 603, Fort Erie, Ontario L2A 5X3

Want to try 2 free books from another series! Call 1-800-873-8635 or visit www.ReaderService.com.

THE WESTERN HEARTS COLLECTION!

19 FREE BOOKS in all!

COWBOYS. RANCHERS. RODEO REBELS.
Here are their charming love stories in one prized Collection:
51 emotional and heart-filled romances that capture the majesty
and rugged beauty of the American West!

Get 4 FREE REWARDS!

We'll send you 2 FREE Books plus 2 FREE Mystery Gifts.

Worldwide Library books feature gripping mysteries from "whodunits" to police procedurals and courtroom dramas.

FREE
Value Over
$20
